THE ELF OF UNION SQUARE

THE ELF OF UNION SQUARE

JAN CARR

G. P. PUTNAM'S SONS
NEW YORK

ACKNOWLEDGMENTS:

With thanks to Nancy Gallt, Nancy Paulsen, and John Rudolph, who shepherded this book into print; to Donna Brodie and all who provide haven at The Writers Room; to Susan Kramer, co-chair of Union Square Community Coalition; and to Ada Ferrer, Muhamed Saric, Paolo Paci, and Jackie Samuels-Jaffee, generous friends and consultants. And a heartfelt thanks of course to Stan and Charlie, who've lived with the Elf—as irascible as he is—from the start.

Library of Congress Cataloging-in-Publication Data
Carr, Jan.
The elf of Union Square / by Jan Carr.
p. cm.
Summary: An ancient, crotchety elf named Hiram and his sidekick, a Norwegian rat named Knut, conspire to drive people away from Union Square Park, while fifth-grader Jack Crain and a reporter for The New York Times, Will Manley, investigate.
[1. Elves—Fiction. 2. Rats—Fiction. 3. Journalists—Fiction. 4. Union Square (New York, N.Y.)—Fiction. 5. Parks—Fiction. 6. New York (N.Y.)—Fiction.] I. Title.
PZ7.C22947El 2004
[Fic]—dc22
2003012739

ISBN 0-399-24180-9
10 9 8 7 6 5 4 3 2 1   First Impression

To Peter, Scott, and Charlie, the guys with the elfin grins.

Contents

1   THE PARK

In New York City, as everyone knows, there are many people. There are rich people and poor people, young people and old people. There are people who come from different countries, people who speak different languages, and people with every shade of skin. Somehow, these people, different as they are, all live and work together in one tightly packed city.

And they all get along.

Or perhaps I should put it this way: They get along *most* of the time.

It helps, of course, that there are parks in the city, places where the people can go to spread out, relax, and enjoy themselves and each other. And in New York City, there are a lot of parks. Some are big, stretching across blocks and blocks of land. Central Park, for instance. If you go to Central Park, you might not guess you are in a city at all. It has places that are quite secluded, where you can feel almost as if you have been lost in a wood, a wood as deep and dark as any you would read about in a fairy tale.

But other parks in the city are smaller, much smaller, pocketed into the concrete. Small as they are, these parks manage to be green in summer, gold in autumn, white in winter, and colorful with blossoms in the spring. They are neighborhood parks, and people who live or work nearby stop in them to eat their lunches, read their newspapers, play with their children, or do any number of things that people who live in the city take a bit of time to do.

One of the small parks, small but significant, is Union Square Park.

Now, among the people who frequent Union Square is a homeless man, a man with corkscrew curls and nut-brown skin who answers to the name of Lincoln. Lincoln stands at the north entrance to the park, not far, as it happens, from one of the park's statues, the statue of Lincoln—Abraham Lincoln. Perhaps that is how Lincoln came by his name. Or perhaps it is coincidence. The first Lincoln, long dead, is exalted enough in the eyes of the community to merit a statue. And the second? Though alive, he's sunk a bit low in his fortunes, with not so much as a roof to shelter his head from the rain. This Lincoln can be found in the park on any given day, leaning against the fence. Almost as if standing there is the job with which he's been entrusted.

Despite being homeless, Lincoln is well dressed and well groomed, with a ready smile and a neatly trimmed beard. Not bad looking, actually. People who haven't seen him before think he is merely being friendly when he calls out to them as they pass by. But mothers who wheel their strollers to the playground know that sometimes they must hurry their children past. For sometimes Lincoln starts cursing, or ranting about this or that, saying things the mothers would rather their children didn't hear. Though most of the things Lincoln shouts out are quite harmless indeed.

For instance, Lincoln likes to shout out some nonsense about an elf he claims he has seen, an elf who he says lives in the park, whom he intends to get back at, yes sir, because of some offense, some nasty prank this elf supposedly played on him. Something about his shoelaces.

"Curse you, wretched elf!" he shouts.

At which point the mothers speed up and shepherd their children past in case Lincoln actually *does* start cursing. Though they smile at each other as they do. For no one takes Lincoln too seriously. As anyone can see, living outside so long has obviously addled the poor man's brain.

But I'll let you in on a little secret. The truth is, there *was* an elf living in Union Square. The elf was a small fellow, small enough to squeeze through a chink in the ornately carved base of the flagpole that stands in the center of the Square. For it was inside the base of that flagpole that the elf made his home.

And this elf would soon cause trouble, more trouble than anyone in Union Square had seen for a long, long while.

Now, of all the people who frequent Union Square, Lincoln was the only one who'd ever seen the elf. As I said, the elf was small. And camouflaged. His clothes were green and brown, which blended in nicely with the colors in the park—the grass, the ground. Even the cap he wore, a tiny, tasseled stocking cap with a droopy pompon frizzling off the end, was striped a mottled green and brown. The elf could be mistaken—easily—for a piece of a branch broken from some old, gnarled tree.

And gnarled he was. For the elf was old. Very old. He'd lived in Union Square for as long as the Square had stood on that ground. And before that? Who knows? Elves can live very long lives.

Perhaps it was because he was so old that the elf was so crotchety. And had so many complaints about the park. For instance, he did not like the people who sat on the lawn—*his* lawn, the lawn that surrounded the flagpole. The lawn was fenced in, well kept, the centerpiece of Union Square. And it was there that people liked to sun and sprawl and even smooch.

Ptooey!

At the very thought of smooching, the elf would spit. As if casting a terrible taste from his mouth.

Neither did the elf like the playgrounds. And Union Square has three. One is for the littlest children, the second is for children who are a bit older (and therefore likely to mow down the littler ones), and the third playground is simply a sandlot with a jungle gym preferred by some families because of the shade provided by a scattering of old, accommodating trees.

"They like trees so much?" the elf would grumble. "So why don't they move to the country?"

And then there were the dogs. The elf *hated* dogs. The dogs came to the park to go to the dog run, and if you don't live in a city, you might well wonder—what in the world is a dog run? Quite simply, a dog run is a place for dogs to run.

Which city dogs don't get much of a chance to do. City dogs spend most of their day cooped up in apartments, and when they do go out, they are tied to leashes, with which they pull their owners down the street so that they might get to the next fire hydrant just that much faster. But Union Square has an area in which people who own dogs can unhook the leashes. And then the dogs can run, bark, sniff around, and generally go about the happy business of being a dog.

Happy business. That was the crux of the problem. The elf could not abide anything that might be called "happy business."

And so of course the elf hated the restaurant, Fare in the Square. It sits in the park as well, at the top end. The restaurant is outdoors, with no roof or walls—"open air," as they say—so in the summer Fare in the Square is a busy place where waiters carry trays laden with sloshy summer drinks and deliver them to tables of wide-eyed diners, all hungry to hear the list of that day's specials.

"Might I recommend the market tomato bisque. Made fresh from Greenmarket tomatoes."

This sort of talk is enough to send the elf into a rage and turn him as red as a bowl of the bisque, one of the restaurant's more popular specials, made from tomatoes bought locally at the Union Square Greenmarket.

Which brings us to the subject of the Greenmarket. Four days a week, farmers from upstate arrive in their trucks and set up stands for people in the city to buy their produce—juicy peaches, crunchy spinach, bright bunches of flowers, and eggs still warm and feathery from the hens.

"Too many farmers," complained the elf. "Too many flowers."

Why, the fragrant scent of the basil alone was enough to send him retching.

And as if all this didn't make the park irritating enough, underneath Union Square rumbles a subway station. All day and all night long, people who have traveled on the subway climb up the stairs, out of the station, and stride through the park on their way here, there, or wherever.

The elf did not like the hordes of people climbing in and out of the station, traipsing through the park—*his* park. He did not like the Greenmarket. He did not like the restaurant, or the dog run, or any of the three (three!) playgrounds.

And now, as if the situation weren't bad enough, someone had posted a sign. A sign announcing that the park was going to be renovated, that things were going to get better. Which meant, of course, at least for the elf, that things were definitely going to get worse.

The elf liked the park the way it used to be. Years ago. Run-down and dirty and a little scary, frankly—scary enough that not many people ventured in, even during the brightest of the daylight hours.

Oh, the elf remembered those days, all right. And he would tell you about them, tell anyone who was willing to listen. Which is exactly what the elf was doing now, just as our story begins.

2   THE PLAN

"You shoulda been here thirty years ago," the elf was saying. "Those were the days. The heyday, as far as I'm concerned."

The elf was squeezing through the fence to the dog run. There were no dogs there, or people, for that matter, since it was the dead of night. The elf was talking to a rat, a very young one.

"You woulda liked it here then," he said. "There were a lot more of you guys then. Rats, I mean."

"Really?" said the little rat. He had a high, reedy voice and a quick, giddy tail. "More rats than *now*?"

The little rat was amazed by this fact. For though the park had been cleaned up, it was still home to quite a large number of rats. All his uncles and aunts and cousins lived there. Far too many to count.

"Wise up, kid," said the elf. "Your population's down. Back then, you guys used to run the place."

"So where were all the people?"

"Afraid to step foot in the place."

"Aw, come on. You're kidding me, right?"

"Back then, there was some unsavory business going on in

the park. The few people who did hang around here had knives. And guns."

"Knives?" The little rat scrambled to keep up. "Guns? What were they up to?"

"No good," said the elf. He laughed. A mean, nasty laugh. "And of course, the park had a lot more homeless guys back then."

The little rat eyed the elf, trying to figure him out. "So what are you?" he asked. "One of those do-good types I've seen around? Some kind of advocate for the homeless?"

The elf laughed again.

"Advocate for the homeless! That's a good one! Oh, sure, I like the homeless, all right. They were loads of fun when they slept here. Sprawled out on benches, scrounging for food in the garbage cans . . ."

The rat couldn't help noticing that the elf himself had just climbed to the rim of a garbage can, and looked as if *he* were about to scrounge around inside.

"Hey," said the elf, "wanna hear about the time I tied a homeless guy's shoelaces together?"

"Sure," said the rat. He scampered closer to listen.

"I did it when he was sleeping. And when he woke up? He stood up and tripped over his own two feet. The best part was, he thought the guy sleeping on the bench next to him did it. So the two got into a fight. A beaut of a fight. I tell you, it was a joy to behold."

The elf sighed. "But that was the old days," he said. "Like I said, the heyday. Things have changed so much since then, it might as well've been a thousand years. Take a look at the place. In the daytime, it's swarming with people. And it's only gonna get worse."

"How do you know?" asked the rat.

"Ain'tcha seen the sign?"

"What sign?"

"What'samatter? Can'tcha read?"

The little rat looked aside sheepishly. "Reading?" he said. "It's not exactly a rat thing."

The elf pointed to a sign posted just outside the dog run. "It says they're gonna fix up the park even more. 'Renovating,' they call it. Which means that pretty soon they're gonna have bulldozers in here. Construction guys. Making everything pretty as a postcard. Well, that's the last straw for me. There's only so much an elf can take."

The elf reached into the garbage can and pulled out something. He put it in a plastic grocery bag he held in his other hand.

"But I got a different plan," he said. "Things are gonna get *worse* around here this summer, not better. This park is on its way back down, if I got anything to do with it. By September, I'm gonna have this park just the way it used to be."

"More rats?" The little rat's tail twitched excitedly. "How are you going to fix that?"

"I got my ways," said the elf.

The elf reached back down into the garbage can. Again, he pulled out something, and again, he dropped it into his sack. Whatever it was, it smelled bad.

"Pee-yoo!" cried the little rat. "That's some stinky garbage!"

"It's not garbage," said the elf. "It's poop. When the little doggies are in here, running around their little doggy run, their owners gotta clean up after them. And when they clean up, they throw it in here. The poop can. Convenient, wouldn'tcha say?"

"But what are you going to do with it?"

The elf chuckled. "That's for me to know and you to find out."

The little rat watched the elf as he filled his sack with old, smelly poop. He watched him as he hopped down from the garbage can, the bag slung over his shoulder like some kind of Santa Claus gone wrong, and headed out of the dog run. He watched the elf as he reached into the sack and dropped a piece of poop on the walkway right outside.

"Hey!" called the rat. "Wait! We never introduced ourselves. My name's Knut."

The elf looked back. "Newt?" He snorted. "What kinda name is that?"

"It's Norwegian," the little rat said proudly. *"Rattus norvegicus.* I'm a Norway rat. Like most of the rats around here. Our forefathers came over many years ago on boats that docked in the New York harbor. We have a long and proud heritage of—"

"Enough with the history lesson!" shouted the elf. "I asked about your name, not your whole family tree!"

"So who are *you?"* asked Knut.

"Ain'tcha heard?" said the elf. He nodded over to the entrance of the park where, during the day, Lincoln stood rant-ing. "I'm the Elf. The Elf of Union Square. But you?" he said with a nasty smirk. "You can call me Hiram."

And then the elf went about his business, the business of strewing patties of dog poop throughout the park, on the walkways that led through Union Square.

3 THE POOP

There is nothing more satisfying for a crotchety old elf than waking up early in the morning and seeing lots of people rushing to work, hurrying through the park, only to find that they've stepped in dog poop. Hiram had worked much of the night scattering dog poop around the walkways that ran through the Square. Now he watched as people happened upon it—which is just another way of saying that they stepped in it.

Hiram watched one woman, a woman in high heels on her way to her job as a photo editor at a fashionable magazine, step smack into his trap, the spike of her heel piercing the poop as cleanly as a spear. Another, a man on his way to his job downtown counting money on Wall Street, squished the poop all over his expensive shoes. And a third person, this one a fellow wearing sneakers, lifted his shoe to discover that the poop had smashed deep into the grooves of its sole. The fellow sat down on a bench, picked up a stick, and started up the unpleasant business of scraping the whole mess out.

Hiram, who was watching the scene from behind the leaf of a plant nearby, had difficulty suppressing his laughter.

While the fellow in the sneakers was scraping his shoe, a woman hurried by with a boy. Hiram had seen these two before, though usually the boy was on a skateboard. Both were on foot now, both were wearing sandals—Hiram smiled at the unpleasant possibilities *that* presented—and as they rushed forward, both stepped directly in the poop. After which they grabbed seats on the bench next to the fellow in the sneakers. The mother dug a wad of tissues out of her purse and handed some to her son before beginning to clean her own shoes.

The fellow glanced at the woman. She had green eyes and dark hair that she'd pulled back in a springy ponytail. She was pretty.

"They say it's good luck," he said with a smile.

The woman looked at him. Was this man talking to *her*?

"Dog poop," the man continued. "Stepping in it. They say it's good luck."

"Good luck?" she scoffed. "Jack and I are going to be late. I can't be late. The last day of school? My class is going to be climbing the walls."

"School, huh?" the man said. He winked at Jack. "Let me guess. Fifth grade?"

"Fourth," said Jack. "I'll be in fifth in the fall."

"So I was right," said the man.

The woman spun around to face him. "Listen," she snapped. "Can't you see I'm trying to do something here? We're in a hurry!"

She grabbed Jack's shoe to inspect it.

"Mom!" cried Jack. "Yuck! You just wiped poop on my toe!"

The man grinned. "My name's Will," he said. "Will Manley." He stuck out his hand.

The woman did not shake it.

"I don't mean to intrude," the man went on. "I guess I'm just the curious type. Naturally curious. All part of the job, I guess. I'm a reporter. For *The New York Times.*" He looked at them to see if they were impressed.

The woman glanced at the man's clothes. At his worn sneakers. At his T-shirt, which looked dingy.

"Oh, yeah?" she said. "And I'm the Queen of Sheba."

The woman stood up. "Come on," she said to Jack. The two of them hurried off again across the park in the direction of the subway, this time keeping a careful eye on the path where they stepped.

From behind the cover of the leaf where he hid, Hiram watched, pleased. That mom-boy duo? There was something particularly satisfying about snaring those two. Oh, yeah, baby! This was what he loved. This was what he lived for. Putting people in bad moods. Setting them to arguing.

Inspiring people to be just as nasty-tempered and as crotchety as he . . .

Late that night, sack in hand, Hiram made his way back to the dog run. Knut ran beside him, his little rat legs scrambling to keep up.

"Are you going to do it again, Hiram?" he asked.

"Well, I ain't selling Girl Scout cookies."

"Why are you going to do it again?"

14

"Why you think, you pipsqueak?"

"Because there's nothing like the stink of poop in the morning?"

"And the sweet sound of anger all afternoon."

"Who was angry?"

"Ain'tcha got ears? Who *wasn't* angry? I got everybody in the park muttering about the dogs. Disparaging them right and left."

"Disparaging them, huh? Cool." Knut twitched his tail. "What's *disparaging*?"

"What, do I gotta teach you everything? Calling them things. 'Mangy mongrels.' 'Yappy mutts.'"

"Those dogs are loud, aren't they? Do they ever stop barking?" Knut adopted a fighting stance. "Stand back, Fido. I got a set of sharp teeth, and I'm not afraid to use them!"

"Hey," said Hiram. "You know that kid, the one with the skateboard?"

Knut grabbed up his tail and cradled it. "That kid nicked my tail once!"

"Well, I got him."

"All right!" cried Knut. He snapped his tail, whip-like. "Let's get him again!"

"In due time, kid. In due time. I got a lot more on my list than one scrawny skateboarder. The more people around here I get ticked off, the better. I got plans. Big plans."

"What're you aiming for?" Knut asked hopefully. "World domination?"

"Right now I'd settle for park. You know that lady runs the place?"

"Sure. I know her. All the rats know her."

"Well, I got her, too."

"Score!"

And so it went in Union Square. During the day, jackhammers and cement mixers broke up old cement and laid down new. But as night fell, Hiram kept up his own work, his own dirty work. His own dogged routine.

Days passed. Days turning into weeks. Over time, people in the park began to feel fed up with the dogs. Fed up with the telltale, squishy feel of poop underfoot. Fed up with scraping poop off their shoes. It tested their usually friendly and polite New York demeanor. And soon enough, they were not only muttering their displeasure, they were shouting it. Directly at the dogs. Or, I suppose it would be more accurate to say, at the people who held the dogs' leashes, the ones parading past with their pups.

"Clean up after your mutt, why don'tcha!"

The first of the dog owners to be yelled at just stood there. Blinking. Didn't he always clean up after his dog? And hadn't he just done exactly that?

But the second person to be yelled at decided, as is only human, to yell right back.

"Aw, blow it out your nose!"

And the third did even worse. She let up on her dog's leash. Just enough for her dog to pull. Just enough for the poodle—petite and pomponed though she was—to give a fright. And the owner herself to growl, *"Sic 'em, Foo Foo!"*

Tensions in the park had begun to run high.

■ ■ ■

"Easiest job I ever done," boasted Hiram. "I'm telling you, this job is a piece of cake."

Knut tagged along, his step not as sprightly. "But aren't you getting tired of it?" he asked. "I mean, we've been doing this a lot of nights here. It's starting to feel old already."

"What're you, kidding?" said Hiram. "I ain't gotta do nothing. Toss around a little doggy dirt. Give people a little nudge. Then all I gotta do is sit back—put my feet up if I want—and watch as those morons themselves, *of their own accord!,* go at each other tooth and nail. Hey," he said, "didja see those signs people put up? The ones over by the dog run?"

Knut scratched the ground self-consciously. "What'd they say?"

"MUZZLE YOUR MUTTS! was one."

"That's funny."

"IMPOUND THE HOUNDS! was another."

"Clever, clever."

"And I hesitate to tell you what else."

"Aw, come on!"

Hiram looked the runty little rat up and down. "Nah," he decided. "You're too young. I draw the line at corrupting minors."

As fate would have it, Hiram and Knut were not the only ones to take note of the signs. The day they appeared, Will Manley, the reporter, had returned to Union Square. He'd come snooping back around to check up on the place, sniff

17

out developments there. And when he read the signs, he winced at the sentiments, almost as if the sour smell of the poop that inspired them had wafted up and assaulted his nostrils.

He copied the messages into his notebook. As he did, a young woman, spike-haired and spark-eyed, stepped up to him. She thrust a clipboard into his hands.

"Sign our petition!" she urged.

"What's it for?" Will asked her.

"We want the Parks Department to get rid of the dog run," she said. "We're demanding that they ban dogs from the park altogether."

Ban dogs? Altogether? That seemed a bit extreme. "I'll have to think about that," Will said politely.

Will moved on, making a note of all he saw—the nasty signs, the angry petition. And it occurred to him. Maybe it was time for him to write an article. An article about all that had been happening in Union Square.

The next week, the article Will wrote appeared in the paper. On the front page of the Metro section of *The New York Times.*

4   PLAN B

In the office of Benjamin Greene, an un-comfortably warm sun pushed in through the window, heating up Greene's desk and the papers that lay all across it. Benjamin Greene was the parks commissioner, a title that simply means he was the person in charge of all the various parks throughout the city (and I think you'll agree that "Greene" is the perfect name for a person in charge of that). Greene folded up the copy of the newspaper he'd brought with him to the office. He picked up his phone and called Celia Fuentes, the woman whom he'd hired to manage Union Square. Celia was, at that moment, unlocking the gate to the center lawn, opening it up for the day. She answered her cell.

"I need to talk to you," Greene told her. "In my office. Come up here right away."

Celia winced. She'd read the article, the one that had ap-peared in *The Times* that morning. So she had a feeling she knew why her boss wanted to speak with her. And Celia was right. When she arrived, and was ushered into his office, the commissioner was on the phone.

"Yes, Mayor," she heard him say. "Bad publicity. No. . . . Of course not, Mayor. I understand. . . . I've got the manager of the park right here."

The commissioner hung up the phone. He glowered at Celia, the muscles in his face tense and taut.

"So what's this about dog poop in Union Square?" he demanded.

"We're not exactly sure how it gets there," said Celia. "Or when." She explained to the commissioner that she and her crew swept up every night. "And then again first thing in the morning at nine o'clock. When our workday starts." Though by that time, of course, many people had already passed through the park on the way to the subway, to get to their own places of work.

The commissioner scowled. "Your solution to the problem, sweeping up at nine—obviously, this hasn't been working, has it?"

Celia didn't like the tone of the commissioner's voice. He was talking to her as if she were a child.

"And when Plan A doesn't work," he went on, "what do you do?"

Talking to her as if she were a schoolchild, and a slow one at that. As if he were the kind of teacher who couldn't even imagine she'd be able to manage the right answer.

"Plan B," she said hesitantly.

"And Plan B is that you clean up earlier. You'll clean up at six."

"Six?" stammered Celia. Did he mean six in the morning? "That sounds awfully early," she ventured.

"Six!" the commissioner shouted. "And no later. I don't want any more bad publicity about Union Square. Understand?"

Celia understood, all right.

What Celia didn't understand was how she was going to solve her own problem, a problem the commissioner wouldn't care about, but one that loomed large for her. Every night and into the morning, Celia took care of her granddaughter. She watched the little girl while Celia's daughter, the girl's mother, worked the night shift.

And if she had to be at work at six, who would watch the girl in the mornings? What would Celia do?

Glumly, Celia nodded her assent to Commissioner Greene and slunk out of the office.

"Ayúdame, Dios mío," she murmured, a phrase in Spanish that means "God help me."

She would think of something, she supposed. She'd have to.

But this was inconvenient.

Very inconvenient indeed.

All the way back to Union Square, Celia worried about the problem. At the Square, she paused a moment near the center lawn, gazing in at the soft, green grass before calling together the people who worked for her. And then, though she didn't realize she was going to do this, Celia yelled at them. Yelled at her staff, who had been cleaning up dog poop so dutifully for the better part of a month.

Maybe you have noticed this phenomenon. It often happens when one person yells at another. Shortly after, that person yells at someone else. And, in turn, that person yells at a third.

Hiram noticed. He crouched behind a bench nearby, enjoying the scene immensely.

"Thatta girl, Celia!" he cheered, loud enough that only he could hear. "Give 'em whatfor! Lay those lowly broom pushers lower!"

"So you'll have to be here by six," Celia informed her staff.

Six? Hiram started.

"The commissioner wants us to get the walkways clean by the time everyone else is going to work," she said.

The cleaning staff groaned. Loudly. Each of them, you can be sure, had his or her own reasons for not wanting to get to work by six.

Celia glanced at the lawn, her pretty stretch of lawn. Though the gate swung wide open, it was still early enough that there was no one yet on the lawn. The expanse of grass was empty. Celia drew a key from her pocket and locked the gate.

"See that this stays locked today," she instructed her staff.

At least there was one part of the park she could keep clean. At least there was one part to lock up.

As Celia stalked off, her staff leaned on their brooms.

"Stupid dogs," one muttered.

And the workers weren't the only ones who were unhappy. The news that they were now to arrive by six was a low blow to Hiram. If the cleaning staff started sweeping up at six every morning, there was no use in his working all night, dragging the poop all about, no use at all. The poop would only be cleaned up before anyone would have a chance to step in it.

Well, this was a wrinkle. A new wrinkle entirely.

Hiram sighed. The old plan had been easy. Like taking candy from a baby. It had been a nice run, but now he'd have to think of a different plan, a fresh way to cause trouble.

Hiram looked around. His eye fell on the playgrounds. On a jungle gym. The red metal jungle gym that rose like a dome from the sandlot. He glanced across the walk at the other playground. That one had more jungle gyms. And slides.

Hiram laughed. A low, growly laugh.

Candy from a baby, eh? That was it! Where did babies play? In the playgrounds!

And Union Square had three. . . .

5

ALL FALL DOWN

It was morning in the park. The dew was misting off the grass, and though it was early, the air was already hot and moist. At the south end of the park, in the half light, some people could be seen padding away from one of the statues there, a statue of Mahatma Gandhi. Gandhi, old and wizened, was draped in a simple cloth, nothing more. He was walking with a stick, caught in midstride. And around his neck hung a necklace of flowers, fresh flowers, placed there, apparently, by the people who'd just passed. They'd given the lei to the Mahatma to accompany him on his journey, wherever it was he was going.

A short way from the statue, the cleaning staff was gathering, early, much earlier than they usually did. It was 6:00 A.M. The staff looked sleepy. In their rush to get to work, they had not had time to enjoy their cups of morning coffee or tea. They'd struggled into clothes hurriedly, in the dark, had crept out of their apartments trying not to wake sleeping children—children who would have to be awakened later by neighbors pressed into service, how long could they be counted on to help? Now, the staff had arrived at work early, as ordered, so they could clean the poop off the walks.

Though that morning, as they discovered, there wasn't any poop on the walks at all.

Odd as it may seem, this discovery did not please the staff. In the past weeks, they'd gotten in the habit of cleaning it up—all part of the job—and if they were going to go to the trouble of getting to work early, they would at least have appreciated having something substantial to clean up when they got there.

Leave it to the dog owners to be so thoughtless, they thought. Leave it to the dog owners to get them dragged to work at the crack of dawn, then neglect to leave anything for them to clean up once they got there.

Hiram watched the staff as they grumbled, as they cursed the dogs and dog owners, as they cursed their boss, Celia, and her boss, Commissioner Greene. Their day had gotten off on just the wrong foot. Though Hiram's day had started off exactly as he'd hoped.

Hiram yawned. He felt tired, really tired. Who wouldn't after working through till dawn?

Though not in the dog run this time.

"Hiram! Hey, Hiram!" It was Knut, scurrying up. "I've been looking all over for you."

"So you found me. So big deal."

Hiram strode toward the flagpole, where he fiddled with a small, loose piece of stone in the base, jiggling it free. He slipped through the chink it concealed. Knut wriggled through the crack to follow.

Inside the chink was a large, dark, cavelike space. Hiram

switched on a flashlight that was cracked, but working. Working well enough at least to shed light on the clutter that lay all about.

"Wow!" exclaimed Knut. "This is one cool place you've got! It's a regular rat's nest in here!"

Hiram's hole was indeed a mess, littered with an odd assortment of things, things he had scavenged over time from the park. Old cans, broken bottles. And a notable number of binkies. Babies' binkies, or pacifiers as they are sometimes called. Each one stolen directly from the fat little fist of a suckling child. Each one a trophy of sorts. The trophy collection of a nasty-spirited elf.

Hiram flopped down on the soft pile of cloth that served as his bed. Over the years, the bed had grown quite comfortable, made, as it was, from bits of clothing he had found. Lost hats, mittens without mates, clothes kicked off by babies in strollers—socks, bibs, sweaters.

Knut jumped on the pile to join him.

"Beat it," snapped Hiram.

"Aw, come on," said Knut, nosing up a mitten. "Can't I hang around awhile?"

"Scram!"

Knut sulked. He slunk off the bed and headed for the chink.

"Hey," Hiram called after him. "Meet me back outside later. At nine."

Nine? "But the people are all there then. That's past my bedti—"

"Don't be late."

■ ■ ■

By 9:00 A.M., people were streaming through the park. People going to work. People arriving. Nannies with strollers wheeling toward the playgrounds . . .

Celia moved through the crowd, inspecting the walks. Oh, no. There was that boy again, the one with the skateboard. Probably headed down to the steps to do, what did they call it, grinding? If she'd told that boy once, she'd told him a thousand times: No skateboarding in the park. Well, if he hadn't understood her before, she'd just have to tell him again.

"Excuse me." Someone stepped in front of Celia, blocking her way.

"Yes?" she asked suspiciously.

"You work here, don't you?" the man said. "At the park?"

"I do. . . ."

"I'm a reporter," said the man. He flashed his press pass. "William Manley. With *The Times.* Maybe you saw the article I wrote about Union Square?"

Celia narrowed her eyes. She'd read the article, all right. Hadn't everyone? But that didn't mean she wanted to talk to him. Commissioner Greene had made it clear. No more bad publicity.

Will gestured to a park bench outside one of the playgrounds. "Mind if we sit down a moment?" he asked.

Celia shrugged as if it were all the same to her. "Why not?" she said flatly. She'd give this reporter no information, no information at all.

The sounds of children playing drifted across the walkway in the sticky morning heat. Will smiled at Celia. He opened his notebook.

"About the dog poop here recently," he said. "Has there been any more incidence of it in the park?"

"None at all," Celia said curtly. "That problem's been solved. As you can see, our walkways are now completely clear."

Will paused. Apparently he was up against a tough customer. He'd interviewed people like this before. People who were closemouthed, people who didn't like to reveal much to a reporter. He'd have to think of another question, one that would nudge Celia to give up a bit more information. Maybe he'd bring up the signs—

Will was just about to do so when a nanny ran out of the playground. In her arms she held a child. The child was crying. Wailing, in fact. The little boy's knees were bleeding, and the nanny ran to the water fountain, where she stuck his knees under a trickle of water to clean them.

Celia jumped up. Rotten luck that this would happen when the reporter was here. She rushed over to the nanny to see if she could help.

"Had a little accident?" she asked.

The nanny had the lilting, musical accent of the Caribbean island where she'd grown up—where, in fact, many of the nannies had.

"He fell off t'e jungle gym," the nanny told her. "But t'is one? He never falls. He's a monkey. Sure-handed. I don't know what happened. One minute he was on his way up, t'e next, he was plummetin' down."

Celia smiled in spite of herself. She liked to listen to the nannies talk, liked the sound of it. It always sounded to her as if their words had been tossed and tumbled by the waves of the sea, so much so that their *h*'s had all gotten sloshed in the surf and washed away.

She pulled a couple of wipes from her pocket and offered them to the nanny, who patted the smeary mess from the boy's knees. Then Celia went back and settled on the bench next to Will. She smiled again. Tensely.

Will glanced at his notebook. Where was he? The signs. That's right, he was about to press Celia about the signs in the park. Though he'd need to do so carefully, come at it roundabout.

"So," he said. "We were talking about the dogs. I'm wondering, have you noticed any more tensions in the park? Tensions, for instance, on the order of those nasty signs people were posting, the ones about the dogs?"

Celia eyed him. How had he found out about those signs, anyway? She and her staff had stripped them down as soon as she'd spotted them. And what did this reporter know now?

Another wail pierced the park. Another nanny ran out of the playground carrying another child, this time a girl clutching her forehead. The nanny ran to the water fountain and cupped her hand to gather handfuls of water, which she poured over the girl's wound. Celia jumped up to see if she could help. *Ay yi yi!*

"The jungle gym?" she guessed.

"No," said the nanny. "T'e fire pole. I can't t'ink why it

happened. T'is girl? She's been slidin' down t'e fire pole since she t'ree. It looked to me like she got hold of it, but t'en I saw she was fallin'."

Celia fished into her pocket again and this time pulled out a Band-Aid, which she handed to the nanny. She glanced at Will. Wouldn't you know? He was taking notes. She made a note of her own, a mental note, one that had nothing to do with the situation at hand, at least on the surface. She would keep the gate to the center lawn locked. She was glad she'd thought to lock it the day before. At least now nothing could happen *there*. Not on her lawn, her pretty, protected lawn. Celia returned to join Will on the bench.

"You were saying?" she asked.

In fact, by this point, Will had forgotten what he'd been saying. Suddenly he was much more interested in the events of the past few minutes, the accidents in the playground.

"Do accidents usually happen here so frequently?" he asked, as casually as he could. "In the playgrounds, I mean?"

"Never," Celia pronounced firmly. "All our equipment has been designed for safety. We have rubber padding on the ground. We follow every safety regulation."

"But how do you explain what's been happening here this morning?" asked Will.

Celia pursed her lips. She had no idea why there'd been so many accidents that morning, though she didn't want to admit that to the reporter.

At this point two nannies, then a third, ran out of the

playground. All were carrying crying children and headed for the water fountain. This time Celia wasn't the only one who jumped up to see what was the matter. Will jumped up as well. Soon all the adults were pouring handfuls of water over the children's cuts and scrapes. One of the children had a gash on her chin that wouldn't stop bleeding. Will whipped out a clean handkerchief, placed it on the wound, and applied pressure, the best thing to do with a cut. Still, her chin bled.

"I think this one's going to need stitches," he said.

"No!" cried the girl. She struggled to get free. "Mommy! I want my mommy!"

The nanny held tight, smoothing the girl's hair to reassure her. "Don't worry, baby," she said, though her own voice sounded scared. "Nellie got you. I'll take care."

Celia ran ahead to the street. She hailed a cab and hustled the nanny and the little girl in. "St. Vincent's Hospital," she instructed the driver. "Emergency Room. Fast."

None of this—not the string of accidents, not the dash to the cab, nor the reporter snooping around—had escaped the notice of Hiram, who crouched with Knut in the shadows nearby. Hiram laughed darkly.

"Wha'd I tell you?" he said. "Didn't I tell you it'd be mayhem in the park as soon as the stroller crowd arrived?"

"So what did you do?" asked Knut. "How did you fix up all the accidents?"

"Simple," said Hiram. "I soaped up the equipment."

Knut stared at him. That didn't sound like the Hiram he knew. "You mean you cleaned it?"

Hiram snorted. "Clean, *schmean*! I booby-trapped the place! I worked all night soaping it up. I got a bar of soap from the bathroom by the restaurant and I soaped up every inch of the playgrounds. The jungle gyms, the slides, the fire pole, the swings. In this humidity? The soap gets slippery. So the kids can't get a good handhold. They climb up with their sweaty little hands and—BOOM!"

And then, as if his little prank was little more than child's play, as innocent as a simple game of ring-around-the-rosy, he grinned. "All fall down!" he sang.

By this time, more grown-ups were pouring out of the playgrounds. Nannies, moms, dads, and grandparents alike, each with a child or two in tow. They rushed past Will and Celia, past the drinking fountain, all going somewhere. Where? Will stopped one of the nannies and asked her.

"I got no idea," she answered quickly. "But we can't stay in t'ere. T'ere's some kind of spirit in t'ere, a bad one. Makin' mischief. All the children are gettin' hurt."

Will walked through the stream of people flowing past him and into one of the playgrounds they had fled. He walked over to the jungle gym and stared at it. Nothing looked unusual. Not to his eye.

A few feet outside the playground gate, Lincoln was shouting. To any who cared to listen. And what he said was not all that different from what the nanny said, that a spirit had visited the playground, a mischievous one. Though

Lincoln had a different name for it, a name he'd shouted before.

"It's the elf!" he cried. "It's the elf who's to blame!"

But Will didn't hear Lincoln, or if he did, he didn't notice. He looked around the playground, wondering. What in the world was happening?

What was going on in Union Square?

6 COOL, REFRESHING LEMONADE

Not too many days later, in an apartment only a stone's throw from Union Square, Jack and his mom were enjoying an unhurried morning. Jack, the boy with the skateboard, and his mother, whose name was Mimi—their last name was Crain—had settled, for better or for worse, into a rather lazy summer. Most of Jack's friends had gone off to camp—some to sleep-away camp, others bused to day camps just outside the city. But this year, Jack had talked Mimi into letting him spend the summer at home. Which, at the time she'd agreed, had seemed like a good idea. Didn't children need some unstructured time, she'd thought, some time to play whatever they wanted, some time to let their imaginations run free?

Now, however, with Jack out of school and she home from work more than a month already, the two had found themselves stuck at home together a few too many afternoons in their rather tiny apartment. And though Jack did not at all wish he had gone away to camp, his mother found herself wishing that he had.

On this particular morning, Mimi had just told Jack to turn off the TV, which he had been watching for a good chunk of the morning. Jack had done so, though he'd complained about it ("But *Sherlock Rocks* is my favorite show!"), and had stalled long enough to see one final commercial. The commercial was for a game cartridge. Something called Avenger's Revenge.

"Mom," said Jack as he turned off the TV. "I really need one of those."

"One of what?" his mom asked distractedly. She was sitting at their table, paying bills.

"Avenger's Revenge. It's a really cool game."

Mimi did not glance up from her checkbook. As far as she could make out, this latest Revenge toy was some sort of cartridge for that little hand-held game player Jack was always carrying around. She vaguely remembered that he'd asked for it before.

"This is exactly why I don't like you watching commercial TV," she said irritably, punching up some numbers on her calculator.

"But everyone at school has it," Jack argued.

Mimi stood firm. "You know we don't have enough money for that. I don't even have enough money to pay the bills. Maybe you could put it on your Christmas list. Or you could ask for it for your birthday."

"Christmas!" cried Jack. "That's almost five months from now! And my birthday's even longer."

"Well, I'm sorry. We can't get it. Those cartridges are expensive. We're strapped for money right now."

Jack frowned. He got out his skateboard and pedaled it down the short, narrow length of living room. As he neared the table, he jumped up, catching air.

"Oh, no," said Mimi. "You can't skateboard in the house. Why don't you take your board to the park?"

"Right. And get busted by Park Ranger Sally?"

"I think her name's Celia."

"Whatever."

Jack stowed his skateboard and took out his deck of Revenge cards. He pulled off the rubber band that bound them and stretched it taut, aiming it idly at his mother.

"Don't you dare," she warned.

He aimed instead at their cat, Bullseye, at the swirly pattern that spiraled out on his side.

"Jack!" his mother protested.

"Just kidding," said Jack. He let the rubber band go slack. "We never have enough money to buy anything," he complained.

"You noticed?" said his mother. "It's called raising a child on a teacher's salary. I hardly ever buy new things for myself," she lectured. "If you look at all the stuff in your room, you'll see that you get a lot more new things than I do. I haven't had a new dress in ages."

Mimi stopped herself from saying more. She knew how she sounded. Unpleasant. Who would want to listen to someone who sounded so unpleasant? Why, she herself wouldn't want to listen to anyone harping away in that tone of voice. It was just that it cost so much money to get by anymore. And sometimes she wondered how they were going to make it.

"What if I earned the money myself?" Jack asked.

"Well . . . ," Mimi considered. "I guess you could get it

then. But how are you going to earn enough money to buy a cartridge? Aren't they forty dollars or so? How would you even earn any money at all?"

"I could have a lemonade stand," Jack suggested.

Mimi looked at Jack. From skateboarding and Avenger's Revenge to a lemonade stand? There was something slightly old-fashioned about a lemonade stand. . . .

"Please," he appealed.

Well, it wasn't a bad idea. At least it would get him out of the house.

"Where would you do it?" asked Mimi. "In front of our building?"

"The building?" he said. "No way. It'd have to be someplace people would really want to buy lemonade. Like the park or something. Union Square."

"I think you need some kind of permit to sell food in the park," said Mimi. "Some sort of vendor's license or something." She ran her fingers through her hair. "But I don't think they'd really get upset about a young boy and his lemonade stand. I mean, would they?"

"Are you saying I can do it?" asked Jack.

Mimi sighed. "Okay," she agreed. "But you'll have to pay me back for anything you need for the stand. The ingredients for the lemonade, the cups. All the expenses will have to come out of what you earn."

"Yahoo!" cried Jack. He aimed the rubber band at his deck of Revenge cards and shot. The cards scattered.

"Bull's-eye!" he cried. "Avenger's Revenge!"

■　　■　　■

A short while later, Jack was in Union Square, selling lemonade. He stood in front of a kitchen step stool, one he'd carried from home that now served as his stand. He'd also made a series of signs, very clever signs if he did say so himself, to direct people to his stand. The first sign said HOT? That one, he'd propped at the end of the walkway leading up to the stand. The second sign said THIRSTY? This, he'd positioned a bit closer. And the last sign, which he'd taped directly onto the front of the step stool, proclaimed in big, block letters, COOL, REFRESHING LEMONADE—ONLY 50¢. On the top of the step stool he'd set a tall pitcher of lemonade, sweat beaded up on the colorful sides of the plastic pitcher, and a stack of paper cups to serve it in.

"Lemonade!" Jack shouted out as people passed by. "Cool, refreshing lemonade!"

Because it was a reasonably warm summer morning, Jack had no trouble finding customers. Before long, a whole slew of people were stopping to buy, and Jack was doing a brisk business. One man even handed Jack a dollar bill.

"Keep the change, son," he said.

Jack grinned and waved the dollar at his mother, who'd come out to enjoy the air herself and had settled on a park bench nearby to read the morning paper. She smiled and waved back.

In a short time, Jack had sold all of the lemonade in his pitcher. He carried the empty pitcher over to his mom.

"All sold out," he said proudly. "I left the other pitcher in the refrigerator. Can you go home and get it?"

Mimi looked at the lemonade stand all set up on the walk. If she went back to the apartment, it would leave Jack alone.

"How about if you go back?" she suggested.

"But I have to watch the stand."

Oh, she knew. If they lived in a small town somewhere, or out in the suburbs, Jack would be running around by himself all the time, why, he'd have been doing it for years now. But for kids growing up in New York City? Things were different. Jack went out on his own now, but every time he walked out the door, she pictured his face on the side of a milk carton.

Jack Crain. Disappeared child. Last seen in New York City, wandering around by himself. WHAT HAD HIS MOTHER BEEN THINKING?

Mimi sighed. "I'll be right back," she agreed.

"Thanks, Mom!" Jack was already heading back to the stand.

"But Jack!" Mimi called after him. "Whatever you do, don't talk to any strangers."

"Aw, Mom!" Jack looked around to see if anybody had heard. His mom could be so embarrassing! "I've been talking to strangers all afternoon," he said. "Remember? They're called *customers.* I'm running a lemonade stand!"

"You know what I mean."

Mimi headed back to the apartment. Jack took his place at the stand.

Shortly after Mimi had gone, a man walked up.

"Hi," he said familiarly.

Jack didn't recognize the man. Or did he? Did the guy look familiar? Sort of.

"You don't remember me, do you?" said the man. "But I re-member you. You're Jack, aren't you?"

"Yeah . . ."

"The boy who stepped in dog doo? The last day of school? I was the guy next to you on the bench."

"Oh," said Jack. "Sure, I remember. We saw your article in the paper. You're William Manley, right?"

"That's me," said Will. He puffed a bit, proudly. "You can call me Will." He was pleased that Jack had noticed his name. Maybe that meant the boy's mom had noted it, too. That pretty mom. He looked around the park to see if he could see her.

"So," Will said. "You got a lemonade stand going here, huh?"

"Yeah," said Jack. "I want to buy an Avenger's Revenge car-tridge. You know, for my game player. But my mom says we can't afford it. Not unless I earn the money myself."

"So your mom won't spring for the cartridge for you, eh?" Will said, still glancing around the park.

"Nope," said Jack.

"And you can't talk your dad into it, either, huh?" he asked.

"I don't have a dad," Jack said simply. "Just a mom."

"Oh," Will said quickly. He brightened considerably when he heard this news. This was exactly what he'd been hoping Jack would say. "I didn't mean to get personal on you or anything. You know. I was just wondering. About that Revenge game."

For a moment Will couldn't think of anything else to say.

"So how about a cup of that lemonade?" he asked. "Fifty cents? That's gotta be the best bargain in town."

"I'm out of lemonade right now," said Jack. "But I'm waiting for more. My mom went to get it. She should be back any minute."

"Any minute, huh?" Will would have to think of a few more things to talk about.

"Hey," he said. "It just occurred to me. You're the perfect person to ask about this. I'm working on a story now. About the playgrounds. And you probably know something about them. Do you play in them ever?"

"The playgrounds here?" asked Jack. He glanced across the walk at one and shrugged. "I used to. When I was younger. The playgrounds in this park are for little kids."

"Did you ever have any accidents there?" Will asked.

"Accidents . . . ," said Jack. "Maybe I did. Once I scraped my knee, I think."

"But you never had a really *bad* accident there?"

"Not really," said Jack.

"Did you ever notice a lot of other kids having accidents?" asked Will.

"Well," Jack considered, "once a big kid ran into a little kid and knocked him down," he offered helpfully. "The little kid cried until the big kid promised he could play with his water pistol." Jack looked at Will. "You know, things like that."

"Well, there've been a lot of accidents in the playgrounds here lately," Will told him. "Serious accidents. See that note someone taped on the outside of the gate over there? One of the nannies posted it. It's warning people not to play there. It says that some kind of mischievous spirit has taken over inside."

"Really?" said Jack. He was not used to adults taking seriously the idea of spirits, mischievous or otherwise. "A nanny wrote that?"

"Hey," said Will. "Would you mind coming into the playground with me and taking a look around? To see if you spot anything different there? I went in a few days ago myself to check the place out, but you know the place better than I do. Maybe you would notice something I didn't, something significant."

"Sure," said Jack. "Why not?"

And so Jack walked off with the reporter, abandoning his lemonade stand.

The gate to the playground banged shut behind them.

7
A SLIVER OF SOAP

That morning in the playground, the first thing Jack noticed was that no other children were there. Despite the fact that it was a warm summer day.

"Wow!" Jack exclaimed. "This place really *is* deserted. It looks like some kind of ghost town!"

Will nodded. "Doesn't it?" he agreed. "But besides that," he asked, "is there anything else that looks different to you?"

Jack started to walk around. Nothing did, really. On the ground Jack saw the remnants of a chalk drawing, a drawing of a stick figure, or part of one. The figure had a head and a torso, but no arms or legs. A drawing that some kid had started, but abandoned. Other than that, there wasn't anything that looked particularly unusual.

Jack walked up to a set of monkey bars, the kind kids work their way across hand-over-hand. He jumped up to grab hold of the first rung and reached out for the second. But as he grabbed it, his hand slipped, and Jack fell to his knees below.

"Yikes!" he said. "Those guys are slippery!"

"Really?" said Will. He reached up to touch one.

"Someone must've polished them or something," said Jack. "They were never slippery like that before."

But the bars didn't look polished. The paint on them was peeling. And cracked.

"Why would anyone polish them?" wondered Will.

Jack started to lift himself from the ground when he saw something. Something on the ground there. Something small. And white. Jack picked it up and looked at it.

"What is it?" asked Will.

"A piece of soap," said Jack. "At least, that's what it looks like."

"Soap?" said Will. He took the piece from Jack, and turned it over in his hands. He sniffed it, then climbed up and sniffed the rungs of the bars Jack had fallen from. "Soap," he repeated thoughtfully. "So maybe it's not a mischievous spirit that's been causing the trouble. Maybe it's a person. Someone flesh and blood."

"What do you mean?"

"Someone soaped up the equipment. So it would be slippery."

"But why would they do that?"

"Just to be mean. Someone who wanted the kids to fall."

"Wow," said Jack. This was a mystery. A mystery fit for a detective. As exciting as any episode of *Sherlock Rocks* he'd seen lately on TV.

As Jack and Will stood in the playground, puzzling over the sliver of soap, Jack's mother, Mimi, trundled back up the walk of the park, walking slowly, so as not to spill the full pitcher of lemonade she was carrying. Her eyes darted to the lemonade stand. Jack wasn't there. She scanned the park, looking for him. She couldn't see her son anywhere.

44

Mimi's heart lurched. Gone! Her son was gone! She knew she shouldn't have left him alone at the stand!

By now Mimi's heart was racing. It felt almost as if there were a bird inside her, its wings whirring against her chest, a bird trying desperately to get out. Mimi looked frantically up the walkways. She looked down. She placed the pitcher of lemonade on the step stool.

"Jack!" she shouted. She ran through the park, calling his name. "Jack!"

Inside the playground, Jack heard his mother. He pushed open the gate and waved to her.

"Jack!" she cried as she ran toward him. "Where were you? What are you doing? Why aren't you waiting at the stand?"

And then Mimi saw the man. A stranger. Jack was with a stranger. Mimi's throat tightened. The stranger must've lured him!

Mimi drew herself up to her full height. She squared her tiny shoulders, trying to look like the sort of woman who could ward off a kidnapper or a murderer. Who knew what terrible thing this man had intended toward her child, her young, innocent boy?

She glared at Will. "What are you doing with my son?" she demanded.

"Hi," said Will. He smiled at her. "Good to see you again, too. How's your summer vacation going? Did you ever get the dog doo off your sandals?"

"Dog doo?" Mimi looked confused. Her heart was still beating in quick, rapid bursts. "What are you talking about?"

"Don't you remember?" said Will. "The last day of school?

The day you stepped in dog doo? I was the one sitting next to you on the bench."

"The reporter," chimed in Jack. "Remember, Mom? William Manley. We read the article he wrote."

"Well, what are you doing here now?" she demanded, her voice faltering. "What are you doing with my son?"

"I'm sorry," said Will. "I didn't think it would cause a problem. I just asked Jack to help me out. I only took him to the playground."

"The playground?" Mimi asked. "Why?"

"I've been investigating something here," Will explained. "There've been a lot of accidents lately. So I asked Jack if he'd take a look around, tell me if he noticed anything different, anything that might be causing a problem."

"We found a bar of soap, Mom," Jack burst in excitedly. "I mean a *sliver* of a bar. Someone's been soaping up the rungs of the monkey bars. Someone who—"

"Jack," Mimi said curtly, cutting him off. "Go back to the lemonade stand."

Jack knew that tone of voice. It was the tone of voice his mother used when she meant business.

"Now," she insisted.

Jack scuffed back to the lemonade stand, blinded by embarrassment. Worst of all, he could still hear his mom. Now she was yelling at Will!

"Who do you think you are?" she was saying. "Walking off with a boy? A boy in a big city, where anyone could hurt a kid. A kid who hasn't developed judgment yet, who doesn't know the difference between someone he should trust and someone he shouldn't. I bet you didn't consider that, did you?"

Will shook his head sheepishly, apologetically, as Mimi continued to yell at him. She yelled at him until, still angry, she ran out of things to say. At which point she tossed him one last withering glance before she huffed back toward Jack's lemonade stand and planted herself on a bench. Though this time, Jack noticed, she took a bench directly in front of him, not at a distance at all.

How mortifying!

Mothers! Who could figure them, anyway? Sometimes when you thought they would be mad at you, really mad, they didn't get upset at all. And other times, when you least expected it, they went berserk-o over the tiniest little thing.

Will followed Mimi, hangdog, and shuffled up to Jack.

"That mom of yours has quite a fiery temper," he whispered.

Jack could not look Will in the eye. "Tell me about it," he murmured.

"Anyway," Will told him. "I'm sorry. I didn't mean to get you in trouble like that." He fished two dollars out of his pocket and handed them to Jack. "Here," he said. "This is for a lemonade. Since I made such a mess of things? Keep the change. Put it toward that Revenge thing."

Jack grinned. At least Will didn't seem to hold it against him that he had a mother who was a total nut job. This time, Jack did not hold up the money and wave it for Mimi to see. He pocketed the bills. Quickly.

Will winked at Jack and downed his lemonade. As he

headed off, Jack thought of the playground. Of the soap they'd found by the monkey bars. A mystery, a real-life mystery . . .

Jack hefted the pitcher his mother had brought back. Another twenty cups or so. That would mean another ten dollars.

He plucked a cup out of its stack and waved it high at the people approaching him on the walkway. People looking hot. And thirsty.

"Lemonade!" he shouted as loudly as he could. "Cool, refreshing lemonade!"

8 MADAT

Elsewhere in the park, a woman pulled a stack of papers out of a bag. This woman, whose name was Ginger, was efficiently turned out in a sleek linen suit that somehow managed to look crisp and businesslike despite the heat. Ginger looked over the papers in the stack.

Yes, she congratulated herself, the flyers were in order. She had even come up with a name for the group, one with a catchy acronym to boot. And now there it was, emblazoned across the top of each page, in big bold letters no less: MOMS' AND DADS' ACCIDENT TASK-FORCE. MADAT for short.

Ginger peeled one of the flyers from the pile and pushed it toward a passerby. "Emergency meeting!" she said. "About the playgrounds. We're MADAT and we're meeting at noon at the south end of the park!"

One of the people who happened to walk by was Will. He took a flyer.

What luck, he thought. Maybe this woman would have more information about the accidents. Maybe she'd have just the information he'd need to write another article about the Square.

Will made his way down to the south end and sat down

to wait on the steps. A crowd started to gather. Before long, Ginger arrived, taking her place at the top of the steps. She addressed the crowd.

"I've called you all together today," she said, "to discuss the disturbing events that have been happening in the playgrounds. I myself was unaware of these events until this very morning when Hyacinth, the nanny for my children, that is, mentioned them to me. She told me that in the short space of one morning's time, a string of accidents occurred—one child even requiring stitches! And the situation has forced the nannies and children to abandon their beloved playgrounds altogether."

Here, Ginger paused a moment to look suitably sad.

"So," she said, looking out at the crowd. "Has anyone here contacted the Parks Department?"

One women raised her hand, a mussy-haired woman with a long shaggy braid. "We have," she reported, "but the Parks Department hasn't been much help. They didn't really know anything about the accidents, not until I called them."

"And you had face time with a parks official?" asked Ginger.

The woman blinked at the question. *Face time?* She could figure out easily enough what that phrase meant. Obviously it meant meeting with someone face-to-face. It must be the way people in business suits talk at business meetings, she thought uncomfortably. She herself had not been to a business meeting in a very long time.

"No," she answered hesitantly. "I spoke on the phone with someone."

"Someone high up?" Ginger asked.

The woman's face flushed. "Probably not," she admitted. "I spoke with the person who answered the phone."

Ginger grimaced. The person who answered the phone? That was a laugh! She herself would never have wasted her time talking to some underling. When you needed to accomplish something, you demanded to speak to the person in charge. And get face time with him, at that. Didn't everyone know that? Well, apparently they didn't.

It was a good thing she'd come to the park that day to take charge, she thought. A very good thing indeed.

"In my short time here," she went on, "I've had time to assess the situation. And I've determined the cause of the accidents."

Will sat forward. Did she know about the soap?

"The problem," she said, "is that the playgrounds are too crowded. There are too many children playing in them at the same time. I'm not in the playgrounds often, of course. My work just doesn't allow it. But I came one weekend a month or so ago, and I was shocked to see how crowded it was. It's a wonder our children don't have *more* accidents."

"But the playgrounds have been crowded for a long time," said the mother with the shaggy braid. "And there've never been so many accidents before."

"So what we will do," Ginger continued, as if the woman had not spoken at all, "is demand *more* playgrounds."

"More?" The crowd murmured. This seemed a little pushy.

"But we already have three," someone offered.

"They're renovating the park right now, aren't they?" said

Ginger. "And reorganization always presents opportunities for growth. Why not ask for more?"

"But where would they put another playground?" someone asked. "There's no other space in the park."

"Of course there is," said Ginger. "There always is. The dog run, for instance. People are angry at the dogs right now. Which makes the run particularly vulnerable to a takeover. It shouldn't be hard to get the Parks Department to agree to eliminate it altogether. And then they could convert the space into a playground."

No one in the crowd knew quite what to say to this suggestion. For one thing, some of them had dogs themselves and actually used the dog run. One, the mussy-haired one, had even met her husband there. In the days when she was younger and better groomed, she had flirted and her husband had courted her while their dogs chased merrily around the run. . . .

"Maybe we just need some new playground equipment," this mother suggested.

"So it's settled," said Ginger, ignoring her. "We'll petition the Parks Department. We'll get them to agree."

Just up the walk from the meeting, Jack sold his last cup of lemonade. There was a small swallow left in the pitcher, which he poured into a cup and drank down himself. He laid out his money on the top of the step stool. A lot of quarters, some nickels and dimes. He sorted the coins and started counting. Twenty-two dollars!

Jack grinned. Now, that was respectable. He hadn't made

quite enough for an Avenger's Revenge cartridge, but he was well on his way.

As Jack started to fold up the lemonade stand, he noticed a flyer on the ground in front of him. A flyer advertising a meeting, a meeting about the accidents in the playgrounds. Jack picked it up and read it. The meeting was happening right now!

"Mom!" he cried. "Watch my stuff, will you?"

Jack didn't wait for an answer. Before Mimi could protest, or even register what he'd said, he'd sprinted toward the south end of the park.

By the time Jack arrived, the meeting had wound down, and people were already dispersing. Jack saw Will talking to someone, some no-nonsense-looking woman in a suit. Jack ran up and interrupted.

"Did you find out anything more about the accidents?" he asked Will, breathless. "About who's been causing them?"

"Not much," said Will.

"We've already determined the cause," said Ginger, turning to Jack. "The playgrounds are too crowded. We're going to demand that the Parks Department build another."

Jack looked at Will. "You didn't tell her about the soap?" he asked.

"Soap?" asked Ginger.

Will flinched. He hadn't told her about the soap. Reporters liked to get information, not give it.

"We found a piece of soap earlier," Will admitted. "In the playground." He pulled the sliver of soap out of his pocket and showed it to her.

She furrowed her forehead. "So what in the world does soap prove?"

"That somebody soaped up the equipment," Jack said excitedly. "To make it slippery! That's what caused the accidents!"

Ginger took the soap from Will and held it in her hand. She ran her finger across it.

"Who would do such a thing?" she asked. "Who would soap up a playground?"

"Someone fairly disturbed, I imagine," said Will.

Not far from them, Lincoln was roaming about restlessly. He looked agitated, even more so than usual. He was flailing his arms as if they were part of some sort of wild dance. Ginger's eye fell on him as Will flipped open his notebook.

"I'm a reporter," Will told her. "For *The New York Times.* And I'm hoping to write up the meeting you had here. Can you tell me how your organization started?"

"I'd love to," said Ginger, her eyes still trained on Lincoln. "But I need to take care of something right now. Call me at the office later." She fished in her purse. "Here's my card."

And with that, Ginger marched off, striding purposefully down the walkway, the heels of her shoes clicking loudly.

Like the quick-quick clicking of a time bomb.

Like the tick-tick-tick before the . . . BOOM!

9

FARE IN THE SQUARE

Knut crouched low, peering around the side of the statue where Hiram had instructed him to wait. Where was Hiram, anyway? Knut hadn't been happy about having to wait for him outside in the middle of the day like this. Oh, no. He was only there because Hiram had insisted. Frankly? At this time of day? With all these people out and about? Knut would rather have been in his rat hole. *Deep* in his rat hole. Sleeping. Or at least lying low. What would happen if someone caught a glimpse of him? Knut shuddered to think.

There'd been a close call just a while ago, when that group walked by. They seemed to be taking some kind of walking tour of the place. One man had been talking, and he'd had lots of interesting things to say about Union Square, about its history. Though one of the people following him, listening, had almost spotted Knut. Still, Knut had to admit, it had been fun eavesdropping. Really, Union Square had quite an interesting history. According to the man who was talking, a lot of theaters used to line the Square, vaudeville theaters. And the Square had long been a gathering site for protest— pro-labor, antiwar. Knut wondered if Hiram knew any of this. Maybe he actually *remembered* it. He'd have to ask Hiram as soon as he arrived.

"Blasted busybody!" he heard someone curse. "Sniveling snoop!"

Knut didn't have to wonder who that was. There was no one else who swore with such passion. Hiram must be back from his mission. Back from spying in the Square.

"Rat-faced reporter!" Hiram muttered as he scrambled up the side of the statue. "That's right. You heard me," he said to Knut. "Rat-faced. Never trust a reporter. They're weasellier than rodents!"

Maybe this wasn't the best time to talk to Hiram about the history of the Square. . . .

"Ah, but that one lady," Hiram gloated. "Oh, she worked herself up into quite a lather. That was a sight worth seeing. Got the idea to have a landgrab for the playgrounds. At the very thought, she was practically frothing at the mouth!"

"Frothing?" said Knut. "What was she, sick or something?"

"Nah," said Hiram. "She just had herself a bright idea—to try to take over the dog run. The only wrinkle in the works is that reporter. He told her about the soap. Him and that kid. They must've found a piece of it I dropped in the playground."

"Well, that's bad news," said Knut. "I mean, isn't it? Maybe they'll figure out it was you."

"No way, José!" said Hiram. He grinned maliciously. "Not if I pin it on somebody else."

Hiram gazed out from his perch atop the statue.

"Do you know where we are, Knut?" he asked.

"Union Square," said Knut. "In fact, just while you were gone, I heard some interesting historical facts you might—"

"We're sitting on top of the world," Hiram cut him off. "And we couldn't be doing it from a better place."

Knut could think of a better place. "Does that mean we can go home?" he asked.

"Do you know what this statue is, Knut?" asked Hiram. "Take a look at it. Take a good look."

Knut looked at the statue that towered above him. He hadn't noticed it, really, only that there were basins jutting from it, little wells where he might crouch and hope he was concealed. But the statue, he now saw, was of a woman. In her arms she held a child. Another child leaned against her.

"No soppier sight, right?" said Hiram. "A mom and her little baby-boos. They call this monstrosity the *Mother and Children Fountain.* Which means that it's the perfect place for us to be right now. Just as I'm about to create a little more trouble for the wee set."

"But you can't soap up the playgrounds again," said Knut. "There isn't anybody left playing there."

"The playgrounds? That was only the first strike. The second strike is yet to come. And believe me, it's gonna be much more subtle. This time, you're not gonna see any of the little kiddos running around with skinned knees or scraped-up chins. Oh, no. Nothing that obvious. But the tide of public opinion'll turn against the brats. Even more than it has. And it ain't gonna be a pretty sight."

Hiram lowered his voice conspiratorially. "Did you notice

where all the kids went when their nannies dragged them outta the playground?"

Knut hadn't. "To another playground?" he guessed. "In another park?" What was that other park he'd heard of? "Washington Square?"

"Washington Square!" Hiram snorted. "You gotta be joking! Knut, kid, take a look around. They're still here in Union Square. Right under our noses. And they've been here all along. The nannies've been taking them to—"

He looked at Knut expectantly, as if waiting for an answer. Knut didn't produce one.

"Fare in the Square!" Hiram trumpeted.

"There's a *fair* in the Square?" asked Knut.

"Not Fair in the Square, you numskull. Fare in the Square. The restaurant, you dimwit! They had to leave the playgrounds, so where else were they gonna go? Couldn't go to the lawn now, could they? Celia's got the lawn locked up tight—just like we like it. So the nannies brought the kids to the restaurant. They get there as soon as the place opens in the morning, and they spread themselves out, taking up all the tables. Then they order their iced teas, and they sit there—*all day long!*—nursing those measly glasses of tea while the kids run around the restaurant, wild as little animals."

Knut smarted. First Hiram had called the reporter a rat. Then he'd called Knut himself a numskull and a dimwit. And now Hiram was saying that the kids were wild as little animals?

But animals *were* wild. They were supposed to be. Knut

bared his teeth and made a wild, growly sound in the back of his throat. He poked his nose around the statue just far enough so he could peer across the park at Fare in the Square.

"Listen and learn, kid," said Hiram. "I pay attention to details. And that's why I'm in the position I'm in today."

Knut wasn't sure what Hiram meant by this last bit. The position he was in today? Up on top of a statue like this, in plain view of whoever walked by and in danger of being spotted? It didn't seem to Knut that Hiram was in that great a position at all.

Hiram started to climb down.

"Where to now?" Knut asked hopefully. "Home?"

"Oh, sure, sure, go home if you want," said Hiram. "Me? I got work to do."

"More work?" Knut groaned. "In the daytime?"

"Knut." Hiram shook his head. "Let me teach you something here. Life is hard, or ain'tcha noticed? Everything you get, you gotta sweat for. Suffer. Ain't nothing never gonna just come to you, drop down outta the heavens for you, la-di-da. You gotta be willing to stick your neck out. You gotta say to the world, 'Okay, you wanna slit my neck? Go ahead. But I ain't gonna make it easy for you.' "

Knut winced at this last part.

"Think about it," Hiram challenged him. "Are you willing to stick your neck out? Is there anything you're willing to die for?"

Die for? Not really, thought Knut. He kind of liked being alive. Though perhaps if the rats could rule again, as Hiram had predicted. Sure, he liked that idea. That might be worth taking a risk or two. Still, a rat had to look out for his own skin, didn't he? It was certain that nobody else would.

"But what if somebody sees you out there?" Knut asked.

"What're you, stupid? You don't never let them see you. You dart in and out of the shadows. You hide behind benches, behind bushes. Ain't nobody never teached you nothing?"

Knut scratched at the statue self-consciously.

"So are you coming or ain'tcha?" Hiram pressed him.

"Well, *where* are you going exactly?"

Hiram looked exasperated. "Where do you think I'm going, you knucklehead? To Fare in the Square!"

Knut hesitated. There was something he wanted to ask Hiram. A question that had been nagging him.

"Hiram?" he asked.

"Yeah?" snarled Hiram.

"Were you always so mean?"

Hiram snorted.

"Well, *were* you?" pressed Knut.

"What's it to you?"

"At first I was thinking maybe you were, you know, like the crusty type. Hard on the outside, soft on the inside. But lately I've got my doubts about the soft side. Were you *born* mean?"

"It runs in the family," Hiram said, sneering. "My forefathers? We got a long and proud heritage ourselves."

Hiram jumped down from the statue's base. He spied something glinting on the ground, in a weedy patch of flowers. The something was shiny. Hiram snatched it up.

A whistle. A toy whistle. Dropped in the park, no doubt, by some irksome, irritating child. Hiram laughed a low hollow laugh. Soon, there would be precious few of *those* left in the park! He turned the whistle over. Sure, a whistle could come in handy.

He pocketed it and continued on his way.

That day, Fare in the Square was, as Hiram had pointed out, crowded with children. Exactly as it had been for some days now. And by this time, the arrangement had definitely gotten on the nerves of the people who worked there. Many of the restaurant's regular customers had stopped coming there to eat. They didn't want to dine in a place where children were running "wild as little animals," as Hiram had described it.

Instead, the tables were now taken up by nannies who bought their iced teas, little more. And you don't have to be a wiz at business to figure out that there wasn't much money to be made at *that*. The waiters and waitresses missed the customers who came in and ordered whole lunches, with salads on the side, and dessert and coffee afterward, customers whose bills totted up to quite a tidy sum, thank you, and who left generous tips on the tables when they left.

That day, to make matters worse, Mr. Porcini, the man who owned the restaurant, had stopped in, expecting to have lunch. Not an ordinary lunch, mind you. A business lunch. He'd invited Benjamin Greene, the parks commissioner, to lunch with him. And the two had something important to discuss—the lease to the restaurant, which was up at the end of the summer. That meant that the commissioner would be deciding soon whether or not to let the restaurant stay.

Surely, reasoned Mr. Porcini, once the commissioner had enjoyed a lunch there himself, once he saw for himself what a lovely place Fare in the Square was, what an asset to Union Square, he would sign a new lease and let the restaurant stay on.

Of course, when Mr. Porcini had arranged this lunch, he had not realized there would be so many children in the restaurant that day. And the children, Mr. Porcini couldn't help noticing, were getting underfoot of the waiters and waitresses. Waiters and waitresses who carried trays of dishes, balancing the trays precariously as they threaded their way through the narrow aisles between tables.

Mr. Porcini glanced around nervously as he waited for Commissioner Greene to arrive. He motioned to the man-ager of the restaurant, Giovanni, a young Italian fellow with a tousled head of hair, one naughty curl straying defiantly down his forehead.

"Giovanni," he said, "what are all these children doing here?"

"Here?" said Giovanni carefully, in the English he'd been trying so hard to master. "The children, they have been here coming. For week one, I am to think. Maybe more."

"They seem to be a little loud," observed Mr. Porcini.

"Yes," said Giovanni dryly. "We have noticed it the same. I tell the nannies. Time and time. *Bambini* must keep at the tables."

"Today of all days," warned Mr. Porcini. "There can't be any problem. Greene is coming."

"Greene?" Giovanni looked at him blankly.

"Benjamin Greene," said Mr. Porcini.

Giovanni raised his eyebrows quizzically. He still had no idea whom Mr. Porcini meant.

"The parks commissioner," said Mr. Porcini. "He hasn't made a decision whether to renew our lease or not. The fate of Fare in the Square is resting on this lunch. Nothing can go wrong. I want no problems today. None whatsoever. *Capisci?*"

"I am understanding," Giovanni agreed.

Just then, as if on cue, two children, a pair of twins who had been running through the aisles, fell. How? Why? Had they been tripped? The two let out two terrible twin wails.

Giovanni strode over, grabbed the boy and girl by their wrists, and led them unceremoniously back to their table.

"Excuse me," he said to their nanny. "These childrens. They are in your charge? Yes? Well, then keep them kindly at your table. We are having a restaurant here. Not a yard for playing."

The children sat down, as requested. But at the mention of a play yard, they glanced longingly at the playground that bordered Fare in the Square, the one where they used to play. Both missed the freedom they'd had there to run about as they pleased, no one telling them to sit down. In the playground they'd been *allowed* to run, *supposed* to climb.

Giovanni glanced at the playground, too. It wasn't that he didn't like children. Far from it. Why, it hadn't been all that long ago that he himself had been a boy, romping about, tussling with his friends. Just a few weeks back, he had actually enjoyed the sounds of the children playing, of the shouts and calls that had drifted over the fence from the playground into the restaurant. Children needed to play. They needed to run. Like puppies. Yes, that was it. Like frisky little pups. But the restaurant wasn't a good place for them. It wasn't a good place for them at all.

Giovanni made another sweep through Fare in the Square, rounding up a few more wayward children and depositing them firmly back at their tables. Job accomplished, he gave a quick nod to Mr. Porcini, who was still sitting at his table, anxiously awaiting the arrival of Commissioner Greene.

Mr. Porcini nodded back. Beside him, in a potted palm, a frond rustled. Was it the wind?

Mr. Porcini didn't notice. He noticed only that the restaurant was ready. Nothing could stand in the way of his luncheon now. Nothing could disturb the important business he had ahead of him that day with Commissioner Greene.

10 FACE TIME

Benjamin Greene, the parks commissioner, glanced at his watch. He had just arrived in Union Square, and he was a few minutes early. That would give him a little time before his luncheon appointment to take a stroll around the park, make a quick, unscheduled inspection. Take a look at how the renovation was proceeding. Look to see if there was any more trouble afoot.

The commissioner spotted Celia sitting on a bench, where she'd stopped just moments before. She was staring at the lawn, *her* lawn, which had been looking even nicer (if she did say so herself) ever since she'd locked the gate to the fence that enclosed it.

"Commissioner!" cried Celia, popping up. Just her luck he'd caught her sitting down on the job. "What are you doing here?"

"I'm having lunch with Porcini," he said, glancing toward the restaurant. "You know Mr. Porcini, of course? Fare in the Square?"

Celia nodded wistfully. Of course she knew the restaurant, though she had never eaten there. It had always been a little too pricey for her pocketbook. She'd often wished, though, that Mr. Porcini would invite *her* some afternoon for lunch, a gesture of goodwill toward the park perhaps, but she was sure, quite sure, that Mr. Porcini didn't even know who she was.

"The park is looking good," said the commissioner, nodding approvingly. "Construction going well?"

"Right on schedule," said Celia.

The commissioner leaned confidentially toward her. "And any more problems with the dog poop?" he asked.

"No, sir," she said. "Once we started coming in at six, we've found no dog poop at all."

Maybe this was a good time to talk with the commissioner, she thought. About what a hardship it had been for everyone—herself, her staff—to arrive so early in the mornings.

"Actually, Commissioner," she said, "I was hoping to talk to you about our hours."

The savory scent of food wafted up from the restaurant. "Yes, yes," he said, his attention elsewhere. He'd realized it was time for lunch. "Call my office. We'll talk sometime soon, I'm sure."

And with that, the commissioner stalked off, stopping only briefly to bend down and pick up a lone piece of litter, a gum wrapper that he made something of a show (in case anyone was looking) of dropping into the trash.

When the commissioner reached the restaurant, he was greeted by a smiling hostess. The hostess ushered him to his table, where Mr. Porcini sat waiting. Mr. Porcini leaped out of his chair.

"Ben!" he gushed enthusiastically. "So glad you could make it!"

A waiter appeared promptly to deliver a plate of appetizers to the table, which the commissioner fell upon with relish.

"Mmm," he said, his mouth full. "This stuff's good. What do you call it?"

"Tapenade," Mr. Porcini said confidently. He leaned back in his chair. The lunch meeting had gotten off to a good start. An excellent start! Perhaps it would be best not to say anything for a while. The best tactic might be to let the commissioner enjoy his food, soak in the ambience, enjoy the many pleasures that an outdoor restaurant situated so nicely in the park had to offer. Eventually, of course, he'd have to bring up the delicate subject of the lease. But he'd be careful how he did that, very careful indeed.

"Porcini," the commissioner said, still chewing. "That's the name of some kind of mushroom, isn't it?"

Mr. Porcini winced. He hadn't expected the commissioner to bring up the subject of his name. "As a matter of fact," he said, "it is. Yes."

"Is that that kind of mushroom they fry up and put on a hamburger bun? I've had that before."

"No," said Mr. Porcini. "That's a *portobello* mushroom. We have them on the menu if you'd like. Ours are marinated in a vinaigrette, grilled lightly with roasted peppers, then served on freshly baked focaccia bread."

The commissioner waved away the suggestion. "Porcini? Portobello?" he said jovially. "How's a person supposed to keep all these mushrooms straight? Hey," he said, as if the thought just occurred to him. "That must've been how you got into the restaurant business. Growing up with a name like Porcini? I bet it gave you an early interest in food!"

The commissioner laughed heartily, as if he'd made a very funny joke. Mr. Porcini laughed along, though he didn't think what the commissioner said was all that funny. The truth was, he hated being teased about his name. He'd been teased about it all his life.

Mr. Porcini handed Commissioner Greene a menu.

"Might I recommend the tuna steak?" he suggested.

Not far from the table where Greene and Porcini were lunching, a woman entered the restaurant. It was Ginger, the mother of MADAT, fresh from a particularly frustrating conversation with a policeman. The insistent brush of her stockinged legs announced her march down the steps.

Ginger had stopped into Fare in the Square to say hello to her children, the rambunctious twins mentioned earlier— her boy, who was named Christopher, and Christie, her girl. Hyacinth, the nanny who cared for the children during the day, had recently informed Ginger that they'd taken to spending their afternoons at the restaurant, a turn of events Ginger approved of entirely.

Why, Fare in the Square was an excellent place for her children, she thought. Educational. Perhaps if they spent time at Fare in the Square each day, they might develop a bit more sophistication about food. They might stop begging her week after week for McDonald's and take an interest in, say, a nice piece of salmon with a beurre and caper sauce.

Why, perhaps, she thought, if they displayed a real interest, she could look into enrolling them in a cooking class. She'd heard that certain of the better cooking schools in the city now offered classes for children. Yes, that would be a wonderful idea!

As you can see, Ginger had come to Fare in the Square that day with high hopes for the education it might provide her children. Instead, she found her children running around the restaurant, wild.

Ginger strode toward Hyacinth, a somewhat impatient woman, who, it should be said, had two young children of her own, though they were not so privileged as these two, she often thought, no, not so privileged at all. Hyacinth got up to grab the twins and marched them back to the table to greet their mother.

Ginger kissed Christie and Christopher hello. Then she opened the menu that lay on the table. She sighed contentedly. It had turned out to be something of a pleasant day after all, hadn't it? Humid, yes. But the humidity seemed to be easing. It actually felt nice to be out in the air. Perhaps she'd delay going back to work just a bit longer. . . .

Of course. Why not? She'd stay on and have lunch here with her children. Wouldn't that be a treat? She summoned the waiter and ordered a glass of wine.

As she was puzzling over the rest of the menu—the lamb couscous sounded fun—her children escaped from the table once again. Ginger didn't make a move to stop them. Nor did Hyacinth. Each assumed, at this point, that the other would take full charge.

The children ran straight to the little fountain that trickled decoratively (temptingly!) in the center of the restaurant, and splashed their hands in the basin. An act that caught the eye of Mr. Porcini, who immediately beckoned Giovanni.

"I thought I told you to keep those kids quiet," he hissed.

Giovanni made a gesture of helplessness.

"And *where* is the commissioner's lunch?" Mr. Porcini demanded.

Giovanni hurried over to the fountain to pull away the children, who by now were gaily splashing water all over the people seated at the tables nearby. He marched the twins back to their own table. It was then that he saw that their mother had arrived.

"Madam," he said in his broken English. "Do these children are yours? Already I have been bringing them here. And now I find they splash. In the fountain. Getting all wet nearby the customers."

Ginger smiled at the handsome young manager with the charming, broken speech.

"Children do like to play in water, don't they?" she said amiably. "It's a shame there's no water for them to play with in the playgrounds here. Don't some of the playgrounds in the city have water for children? Union Square should have some, too, don't you think?"

Giovanni stared at Ginger. Had she heard him? Did she understand that he expected her to *do something* about her children? American women! They could be so exasperating!

Giovanni did not stay to argue with Ginger. He had to get to the kitchen. He had told the chef to put Commissioner Greene's order ahead of all the others, but apparently the entree had been delayed. He had to find out what was keeping it before Mr. Porcini could find fault with him again.

But the twins he'd left at the table hadn't stayed seated long. They'd popped up and begun a game of chase through the narrow aisles between the tables, running straight toward Commissioner Greene's.

Christopher lunged at Christie. "Gotcha!" She lurched into the table, which was set shaking, as were all the glasses atop it. Mr. Porcini grabbed the commissioner's glass, steadying it just in the nick.

He glared at Giovanni, who had just emerged from the kitchen, Commissioner Greene's lunch in hand.

Giovanni set the lunch on the table. He paraded the children back to their mother.

"Madam," he said, his teeth now set in a tight clench. "I have ask you. Keep your children at the table, I say. With this, there is some problem?"

"Oh, dear," said Ginger vaguely. "Were they up again?" She glanced at Hyacinth. Why wasn't her nanny keeping the children in line?

"The children have cause a big problem," said Giovanni. "They *bam!* into table. The commissioner's table."

"The commissioner?" asked Ginger.

"Yes," said Giovanni. He nodded importantly in the direction of the table. "The commissioner of our parks. He is here because of lease. For the restaurant. It is finished. He must to renew it."

Giovanni was surprised to hear himself say this. He didn't usually give customers information about other customers. That was unprofessional. Somehow it had just slipped out of his mouth. The children must have rattled him, he thought. As much as they'd rattled the glassware.

But at his news, Ginger sprang from her chair. The commissioner! Of parks! What good fortune! She shot to the table Giovanni had indicated and grabbed the commissioner's hand. "What a happy accident!" she cried. "We've been hoping to get a meeting with you. No doubt you're aware of our organization? We're MADAT."

Benjamin Greene stared at her. Mad at? Mad at whom? Who was this woman, anyway? And what in the world was she babbling on about? Something about the playgrounds. And some accidents she claimed happened there. Why had she arrived just as that Italian fellow had delivered his lunch to the table? This woman was keeping him from his meal!

"And then," Ginger prattled on, "I heard that you may not be renewing the lease here to Fare in the Square. So it occurred to me—out of the blue, like inspiration! Why not turn *this space* into a playground? It would be an *ideal* space for another playground, don't you think? It would connect the other two that flank the restaurant, and would make one long play space! It might even be nice to keep the fountain. Then the children would have water to play in!"

At the other end of the table, Mr. Porcini's face flamed.

The nerve of this woman! How dare she propose replacing the restaurant—*his* restaurant—with a playground! Mr. Porcini looked around frantically for Giovanni. Someone had to usher this woman away—immediately!

"Mommy! Mommy!"

Christie and Christopher ran up—though neither of the children were looking where they were going, and Christopher ran directly in front of a waiter, who tripped and dropped his tray. The tray clattered onto the floor directly beside Commissioner Greene, a plate of mashed potatoes spattering his pants.

Christopher grabbed hold of his mother's sleeve. And, as if he hadn't just banged full force into a waiter and sent a tray flying, he whined, "Mommy, I have to pee!"

"Me, too!" Christie chimed in.

Ginger signaled Hyacinth. Hyacinth roused herself slowly and ushered the twins in the direction of the bathroom.

At which point Hiram jumped to action. He'd been watching the whole scene in the restaurant, hiding behind one of the restaurant's potted palms. This was the moment he'd been waiting for.

Neatly as a gnat, Hiram darted to the bathroom. He clambered onto the sink, reached up to the dispenser, and started pulling out paper towels, a great quantity of them. These he stuffed smartly into the two toilets, after which he gave each toilet a good flush.

The paper towels were bulky, much bulkier than toilet paper, and they did the trick of stuffing up the toilets, just as Hiram intended. The toilets overflowed. By the time the twins and Hyacinth arrived, water was gushing out of the toilet basins and flooding the floor.

"Yuck!" the children cried. "Gross!"

The two ran back to their mother, who was still chattering on to the commissioner. Though by this time Giovanni had arrived, had taken her by the elbow, and was trying to pull her away.

"Mommy! Mommy!" the twins interrupted. "The bathroom's flooded! It's gross, Mommy! The bathroom's gross!"

Giovanni dropped Ginger's arm and rushed to the restroom. Oh, no. It was as the children described it. Flooded. And gross. He hurried back out, his own anger welling up, and as ready to overflow as the toilets.

"You!" he shouted at Ginger, his English suddenly fluid and fast. "You and your children! They did this! The toilets are all overflowing! Get them out of here! Get your children out of this restaurant now!"

"Uh-oh," said a small voice. It was Christie. She looked down at the front of her shorts. Christopher looked, too.

"Eeeew!" he cried. "Mommy! Christie peed in her pants!"

Giovanni let out a cry of his own. "This is the last hay!"

He ran around the restaurant, waving his arms. At other children, all the children.

"Out!" he shouted. "Everyone out!"

Commissioner Greene mopped the mashed potatoes from his pants. He picked up his fork. Finally. People had cleared from his table. At last he was free to eat his lunch. Ignoring all the shouting around him, he scarfed down his meal. Then he stood up. He was through. Quite through.

Mr. Porcini jumped up to stop him. "About the lease—" he interjected.

The commissioner cut him off. "I'll have to get back to you on that."

"But when?" asked Mr. Porcini.

"I don't know," snapped the commissioner.

"Tomorrow?" begged Mr. Porcini. "The next day?"

"A week," said the commissioner. "Better make it two. I'll let you know in two weeks' time."

Back in his hiding place behind the potted palm, Hiram chuckled. A nasty, churlish chuckle. Once again, his plan had gone well. Perfectly, in fact. But now the commissioner was leaving. And Hiram had one last trick up his sleeve. He scuttled out of the restaurant ahead of the commissioner and tossed a patty of dog poop—just one, that was all it would take—on the walkway right outside. Moments later, when the commissioner walked out, he stepped in it.

He lifted his foot. He looked at his shoe.

"Celia!" the commissioner shouted angrily. *"CE-LI-A!"*

At the far end of the restaurant, Will Manley sat at a table, where he'd settled after the meeting with MADAT.

How had things in the park taken such a bad turn? he wondered. How had everyone in Union Square turned so tense and angry? He tapped his pen on the table, thinking of the nanny he'd stopped that day all the accidents happened.

It was the fault of some mischievous spirit, she'd said. But what about the sliver of soap Jack had found? Suggesting it was no spirit at all, just a mean-spirited person who'd been sabotaging the park.

And this time wasn't it the children who'd caused all the trouble? Those twins? They must've been the ones who'd stuffed up the toilets. They'd been running from the bathrooms just as they'd overflowed.

None of what had happened seemed to make any sense. Will pulled a napkin toward him and scribbled on it.

"These days, there's not a lot of unity in Union Square."

11 THE SPIRIT OF GANDHI

Jack sprawled on the couch and paged through the paper, looking for Will's byline. Before he met Will, he hadn't been in the habit of reading the newspaper. If he had to admit it, the articles in *The New York Times* were still a little hard for him to wade through. But ever since Will had started writing stories about Union Square, Jack liked to leaf through and see if he could spot one. It was fun to follow the articles, kind of like reading all the books in a favorite series. The last article Jack had found, the one about Fare in the Square, had been particularly cool.

Overflowing toilets! Kids running wild! Jack wished he had been there to see that. If he'd seen it with his own eyes, he might've been able to figure out how it related to everything else, all the other things that had been happening lately in Union Square.

Jack turned the page of that day's paper. There it was—Will's byline, another of his articles. This one was about the renovation in the park. Someone had gummed up the brakes on the fleet of construction vehicles parked there overnight. With real gum. Already-been-chewed gum.

Wild, that was wild. Why would anyone do that? In the

heat of the summer, things in the park were definitely heating up.

Jack clipped the article. He'd saved all the articles about Union Square. Maybe they'd be helpful somehow, in a sleuthing sense, provide clues. He imagined himself apprehending a criminal. "Stop in the name of the law!" he'd shout. He pictured himself handcuffing the guy and leading him off to jail.

Though first, he realized, he'd have to tell his mom he was heading back to the Square.

"Mom," he said. "Look at this."

Jack handed her the article. He'd noticed recently that his mom seemed to be softening somewhat when he brought up Will's name. At least when he showed her his articles. She read this one with interest.

"So I'm going to head over to the Square," said Jack. "Check out things there myself."

His mom frowned, disappointed. "Oh," she said. "I was hoping you'd go on some errands with me, help me carry all the bags."

"Errands?" Jack complained. "Bo-ring." He hated trekking all over the neighborhood while his mom buzzed into a deli to restock the milk, or combed the aisles of the pharmacy for cotton balls.

"How about this?" Jack proposed. "I stay in the park while you do your errands. Then you pick me up when you're finished and I help you carry the bags from there."

Negotiating. Jack was always negotiating. Did all kids do this? Mimi sighed. Loudly.

"All right, all right," said Jack. "I'll go on the errands. As long as you make them quick."

Jack and Mimi had to cut through Union Square to get to the supermarket. A knot of people clustered on the walkway, blocking their path. The people seemed to be listening to someone. A tour guide . . .

It was another walking tour of Union Square.

"No, no," the guide was saying, in answer to a question from the crowd. "It's true that a lot of unions have their offices around here. But that's just coincidence. It's called Union Square because two avenues come together here. Because of the union of the *streets.*"

"Union!" shouted a voice.

The group, startled, looked toward the edge of the crowd.

"Long live the Union!"

The tour guide hustled his group past Lincoln. Through the crowd, Jack spied Will.

"Hey!" Jack waved.

Will waved back. "Hi," he said carefully, looking to gauge Mimi's mood. "You two just get here?"

"Actually, we're just passing through," said Mimi. "We're on our way to do errands."

Was her voice less chilly? It might be.

"*Your* errands," complained Jack.

"You said you would help me."

Jack rolled his eyes.

Will looked from Mimi to Jack, then back again.

"Well," he ventured. Should he suggest it? "I'm going to be

here for, I don't know, an hour or so. If Jack doesn't want to go on errands, maybe he could stay awhile with me. You know, while you do your running around?"

"Yes!" Jack pumped his arm. Mimi pursed her lips.

"You probably think I'm crazy even suggesting it," said Will. "Especially after our last encounter."

This drew a smile.

"But what do you say? I have to poke around here, do some observing. I wouldn't mind the company. Jack could help. I promise I won't take him out of bounds."

Mimi considered. Well, she thought, this was unexpected. But maybe it would be good for Jack. After all, it wasn't every day a kid got to hang around with a reporter from *The Times*. A boy without a father, Mimi reminded herself. A boy who seldom had the chance to spend much time around a man. Though part of her wondered. Sure, she knew now that Will was a reporter for *The Times*. But some part of her still thought of him as the guy who'd made off with her son.

Honestly, she chided herself. Sometimes her imagination could be as wild as Jack's.

"Sure," she agreed.

"All right!" cried Jack.

As Mimi hiked off to the store, Jack and Will settled on a bench.

"So what exactly am I helping you with?" asked Jack.

"Tallies," said Will. "Of who's yelling what. A few days back, I tallied seven people yelling at dogs, five dog people yelling back, and one construction worker shouting at a college student."

Jack looked around. The park was quiet, peaceful. No one seemed to be shouting at all. Jack fidgeted, self-conscious, suddenly, to be sitting there with Will. For a long while the two just sat there. Observing the people of Union Square.

"Hey!" someone shouted. Will and Jack looked. It was a man, shouting at a woman. "Clean up after your mutt!"

"Bottle it, buster!" the woman yelled back.

Will laughed. He nudged Jack as he copied down what they'd said. "There's the spirit we're used to in Union Square."

"So do you think we'll catch the culprit?" Jack asked.

"The soap guy?" said Will. "Maybe. Maybe he's here right now. Even as we speak."

"Could be that guy," said Jack, pointing. "He looks suspicious."

"You think?" asked Will.

"Yeah. Look at him. He's shifty-eyed. And what's he hiding there?"

"Where?"

"In that paper bag."

As if on cue, the man they were staring at pulled a handful of potato chips out of the bag and started to eat them.

"Oooh," teased Will. "Po-ta-a-to-o chips. Ve-ry suspicious."

"Hey," said Jack, his eye wandering farther. "Isn't that that woman you were talking to the other day?"

Will looked up. There was Ginger. She was talking to a policewoman not far from where Lincoln now stood. She seemed to be arguing with her. Jack and Will headed over to investigate.

"You need to keep your eye on that man," Ginger was saying. She was nodding toward Lincoln.

The policewoman, whose given name was Charmayne but whose badge introduced her as "Officer DeShields," pushed her cap back on her forehead. "Ma'am," she replied patiently. "We know that fellow. He's harmless."

"That's what the last policeman told me," said Ginger. "Believe me, you're not the first officer I'm alerting. But how can you be sure?"

"He's a known character in the neighborhood," said Officer DeShields. "Everybody knows Lincoln."

"He shouts," said Ginger. "He waves his arms. The man is obviously unstable. It seems entirely likely to me that he'd do something like soap up the jungle gyms in the playground."

Just then, Ginger noticed Will. She grabbed him by the arm, pulling him into the conversation. "This fellow," she said, introducing him to Officer DeShields, "just so happens to be a reporter for *The New York Times.* He found the bar of soap in the playground. Didn't you?" she demanded of Will.

"We did," he admitted. "Actually, it was Jack here who found it."

"Soap?" said Officer DeShields. "I'm not following this. What's the big deal about soap?"

"Somebody soaped up the *equipment,*" Ginger said, exasperated. "In the playgrounds. Which means that somebody has been *causing* all the accidents there." She gestured toward Lincoln. "And I don't understand why any officer of the law I talk to refuses to believe that it's that homeless man."

Officer DeShields took off her cap and smoothed her hair. It had been a long shift. A very long shift. She was looking forward to going home.

"Ma'am," she said. "We'll keep an eye on him. Does that make you happy? But you'll have to go down to the station house and file a complaint."

"Gladly," said Ginger. "And thank you, Officer DeShields, for taking the matter seriously. You'll thank yourself later. When the truth comes out and Lincoln is apprehended."

As Ginger strode off, Lincoln continued shouting. About the elf now. Nothing he hadn't shouted before.

"Poor guy," said Will. "He has no idea he's just been fingered to the police."

But Jack was still staring at Officer DeShields. Or rather, at her cap. At the inside of her cap, where she'd pasted a picture of an angel, an angel helping a child cross the street . . .

"So," Will asked him. "What do you think? Should we check out the west end? Over by the bulldozers? Why don't we go sit by the Mahatma?"

"The Mahatma?" asked Jack. He looked puzzled.

"The Great Soul," said Will. "Gandhi."

"Oh," Jack said quickly. "Right." He didn't want to look ignorant. Not in front of Will. He knew where the statue of Gandhi was, though he didn't know a lot about Gandhi himself. He made a note to ask his mom.

Near the statue, Jack and Will found places to sit. Across

from them, workers were busy pulling out old railings, replacing them with new. Will had to talk loudly to be heard over the din of construction.

"How about that Lincoln?" he joked. "The man looked dangerous, didn't he? *Real* dangerous."

"Maybe he's gonna strike again," said Jack. "Do something worse. Like shout about *gremlins.*"

"We better keep an eye on him," Will said ominously. "That one's a suspect, all right. Or maybe he'll lead us straight to . . . *the elf!*"

While they were joking, Mimi returned, lugging the bags she'd picked up at the store.

"So did you two solve the big crime?" she asked.

"Not yet," said Will importantly. He lowered his voice, playing the part. "But we have some prime suspects, don't we, Jack? For one, we've got Lincoln over there."

"O-o-oh, yeah," Jack played along. "Lincoln. He's bad, all right. Not to mention . . . the elf!"

"Of course, we've yet to *see* this elf," said Will. "Lincoln is the only one who's ever laid eyes on him. But we're following up on that lead. Aren't we, Jack?"

Jack and Will dissolved into laughter. Mimi looked from one to the other, unsure what was so funny. Apparently, while she'd been gone, they'd developed a private joke.

Will said his good-byes. A police car screamed past. Jack covered his ears and turned toward the statue, the statue of the simply clad man leaning on his walking stick, caught in midstride.

"Hey, Mom," he said. "Who was Gandhi, anyway?"

Mimi looked at Jack, surprised. "You don't know who Gandhi was?" she said.

"Well, you told me, I think. And maybe we talked about him at school. He's some kind of holy guy or something, right?"

"Was," said his mother. "Gandhi died. A while ago. Someone shot him."

"Really?" That was interesting. "Why?"

"Why does anyone shoot anyone?" asked Mimi. "In this case, it's a complicated story."

"So what did he do that was so special?" asked Jack.

Mimi set her bags on the ground. She took a seat next to Jack.

"Gandhi lived in India," she said. "A poor country that used to be occupied by the British. The British went in and sort of ran the place."

"Why?"

"Well," said Mimi, "stronger, wealthier countries try to do that sometimes, go into a poorer country and claim it as theirs. They govern the place, make all the laws, police them. And they take the country's resources. The people who live there don't always have a say."

"But why didn't the people fight them off?"

"They did ask the British to leave," said Mimi. "But they refused. So Gandhi advised the people to resist."

"You mean attack?"

"Not violently," said Mimi. "Never violently. Gandhi advised people not to cooperate, not with any laws that were unjust."

"And that worked?" Jack sounded skeptical.

"Yes," she said. "Eventually. The Indian people stood fast."

Mimi leaned down to right a bag that had toppled at her feet.

"Gandhi tried to teach us, teach all of us, not to hate," she said. "He suggested that the only devils in the world are the ones running wild inside our own hearts. And that is where our battles ought to be fought."

Jack shrugged. He didn't understand what was so terrible about fighting, not if what you were doing was fighting back. Sometimes you had to stick up for yourself, defend yourself. India—its people, its problems—seemed a long way away.

A truck pulled up alongside them, a green Parks Department truck. Some workmen got out.

"Excuse me," said one of the men. "But you two are gonna have to move."

"Move?" asked Mimi. "Why?"

"We're takin' down the statue," he said.

"You're taking down Gandhi?" said Mimi. She looked alarmed. "What are you going to do with him?"

"Me personally?" said the man. "I'm not gonna do any-thing, lady. But somebody in the Parks Department is gonna clean the thing up. They got plans. Big plans. Ain't you no-ticed? They're sprucin' up this whole area. So the statue's not sittin' on this scruffy patch of land."

"When will the statue be returned?" asked Mimi.

"When the work is finished," said the man.

"And when will that be?" Mimi persisted.

"Lady," he said, "we're talkin' about the Parks Department. Of New York City. You want answers? Move to Connecticut."

Mimi and Jack stepped out of the way. As they watched, the men strapped the statue and hoisted it onto their truck.

A woman passed by, walking a dog.

"Hey," Jack yelled at her. "Clean up after your mutt!"

"Jack!" cried Mimi. She jumped up to apologize, pulling Jack forward to do the same.

"Why did you do that?" she asked when the woman had passed.

"Why not?" he said. "It's fun. Anyway, I stepped in dog poop, remember? So did you."

Mimi frowned. But she didn't lecture Jack as she thought she would. All she said was, "I think we need the spirit of Gandhi here in Union Square. Now more than ever."

Around them the day had started to fade. Like anything colorful left too long out in the sun.

Mimi picked up her bags, handing some to Jack. "We've got to make one last stop," she said.

Jack groaned.

"Just the Greenmarket. I have to pick up a few last things."

At the Greenmarket the last customers of the day perused the stalls. While Mimi sniffed tomatoes and squeezed peaches for ripeness, Jack distracted himself by staring into the faces of the people he passed. Was this one the culprit? Was that?

Beside them, people were filling big, oversized bags with produce. The people wore T-shirts lettered HORN OF PLENTY, the name of an organization that collected food for the hungry. Horn of Plenty delivered food to soup kitchens, homeless shelters, to all sorts of places that provided food to those in the city who didn't have enough to eat. At the end of the day, the farmers in the Greenmarket often contributed, donating what they had left.

Mimi smiled at one of the people in the T-shirts.

The spirit of Gandhi must be alive here, she thought. The spirit of Gandhi must be alive and well right here in Union Square.

Though Mimi didn't realize that there was something, someone, whom she didn't see. Someone who was sneaking food directly out of the big sacks meant to feed the hungry, and spiriting it away. Spiriting away food for a purpose that was not so charitable at all.

Someone small.

Someone quick.

Someone darting from shadow to shadow.

12 HARUM-SCARUM

A full moon shone brightly in the sky. It was sometime in the wee hours between sunset and dawn. At this time of night there was no one in the park. No one human, at least. But the grassy lawn in the center of Union Square was crowded. Crowded with rats. A sea of rats, more than you can imagine, lived in the Square. Ordinarily, they wouldn't dare to be out in the open, gathered together in one place.

But what a sight it was, the rats all crowded together, one clambering on top of the other, each climbing over the next in order to discuss the question put to them. Hiram stood on the base of the flagpole, gazing out across the crowd like a general surveying his troops. An odd pile of produce towered next to him. The produce, which was rotting, had been hoarded over the course of weeks.

Hiram was growing impatient.

He blew his whistle, the little toy whistle he'd found in the park. The rats stopped clambering and pricked their ears anxiously toward him.

"Rats," he called to the crowd. "I want your answer and I want it now. Are you in or are you out?"

One rat stepped forward. An old, scrawny rat with sparse whiskers and patchy fur that evidenced a number of fights.

"Why should we do what you've asked us to do?" he said. "What exactly is in it for us?"

"A piece of the pie," said Hiram. "Last I looked, the people had the whole thing—the crust, the filling, and the pie plate, to boot. It's a dog-eat-dog world out there. You gotta grab what you can."

"But why should we trust you?" pressed the old rat. "We'd be putting ourselves in peril."

"Believe me," said Hiram. "Anybody knows the risk? It's me. Anybody knows the value of lying low, keeping to the shadows? But if you rats do what I tell you, the people'll be afraid of *you*. So afraid, they'll abandon the park altogether, give it back to you with their blessing. Hide in your holes? No longer. Scrounge for scraps? No more. I'm asking you to do what you wouldn't ordinarily because this ain't no ordinary time. It's a time your children'll remember. And your grandchildren. It's the day you're gonna take back the park."

The rats turned to each other, undecided. Sure, what Hiram promised sounded good. But what about the danger? Should they risk it? Should they follow?

Knut scrambled out of the crowd and clambered up to the base of the flagpole. He stood up on his hind legs next to Hiram and swallowed hard. Geez! All the other rats were looking at him! Could he speak? He'd try.

"Aunts and uncles," he said hesitantly, his voice quavering. "Cousins and neighbors. I can vouch for this elf. This guy really is a rat, in the best sense of the word. He isn't going to lead us astray. If he says Union Square'll return to the rats, it will. If he asks us to follow him out into the open, we ought to."

Knut paused a moment to catch his breath. All the rats were listening to him, rapt. A shot of confidence surged through him. He felt the power that comes from capturing the attention of a crowd.

"Follow the elf!" he cried. "Follow him to where light lurks. To where the hum of human activity threatens to expose us. Hiram is our hope! He will lead us to a glorious rat future!"

The rats were ready. The time was right.

"Hi-ram!" one rat started chanting.

Another rat took up the chant.

And another in turn.

"Hi-ram! Hi-ram!"

One by one, all the rats joined in until their voices, high as helium, rose like scores of black balloons in the dark night air.

Hiram smiled. He scaled the pile of produce and began tossing fruits and vegetables, one by one, out into the crowd. Peaches, potatoes, carrots, corn. Food stolen from the mouths of the hungry. The rats lined up to catch what he threw, clamping the produce in their teeth. And then, as one, they moved out.

It was an eerie sight. Rats, thousands of them, streaming through the park, following Hiram. As if Hiram were the Pied Piper, calling the rats to him, luring them from one place to another. But Hiram did not lure them to a river where they would leap in and drown. He lured them to the restaurant, Fare in the Square, where the rats squeezed through the narrow spaces in the wrought iron gate, coursed down the stairs, and scrambled about the restaurant wildly, running this way and that.

Those who carried food dropped it conspicuously here and there. On tables. On chairs. All across the flagstone floor.

And then suddenly, as quickly as the rats had arrived, they disappeared.

Or had they?

Under the bright light of that night's full moon, one might detect a whisker twitching from behind a potted plant, a tail or two flicking just behind the bar, a gray rump scrunched behind the refrigerator.

When all were hidden, Hiram called out, "Rats! Wait and listen. For the signal from me."

And then, for the rest of that still, breathless night, there was not another sound.

Not a stray squeak nor squeal.

Day dawned. Union Square awoke. The people arrived, trekking through the park on their way to the subway. The nannies and children returned, opening the gates to the playgrounds. These nannies and children, who'd ventured back once it had become clear they were no longer welcome in the restaurant, had been glad to find themselves back where they belonged. And glad as well to find that the mis-chievous spirit who'd taken such an interest in the playgrounds now seemed to be far away. The sounds of children at play once again filtered through the fences and drifted through the park.

This, of course, pleased the restaurant staff. As they arrived at work that morning to set up, they were glad to hear the shouts of the children. Though they were distressed when they looked around the restaurant and saw the mess someone had left there. Someone had scattered a great quantity of food around, fruits and vegetables in various stages of decay. Fruits and vegetables that had obviously come from the Greenmarket, now moldering in Fare in the Square.

Well, they shrugged their shoulders, there was nothing left for them to do but tidy up. They swept the restaurant clean—cleaner, in fact, than it normally was. For today was the day that Commissioner Greene was scheduled to return, the day he was to deliver his decision—would he renew the lease to the restaurant or not? It was a nuisance, of course, that they had found such a mess when they arrived, but the staff worked quickly and carefully, sweeping up and scrubbing down. Truth be told, they were happy as they worked. Happy scurrying about, getting the place ready for company.

Outside the restaurant, others were busy sweeping up as well. Celia, too, had caught wind of the news that Commissioner Greene was expected back. Back in *her* park, the park *she'd* been given charge of. And she was determined that, on this visit, nothing would go wrong. She glanced wistfully at the menu displayed at the restaurant's gate. She gazed, just for a moment, into the restaurant itself, where waiters were now setting the tables with vases of colorful garden flowers, flowers that seemed to beckon her, the scene as pretty as a painting, one she wanted to enter.

Celia shook off her daydream. She ordered her staff not only to sweep, but to hose down the walkways. She couldn't afford a situation like last time, when the commissioner had stepped in dog poop just as he had been walking out of his lunch. No, nothing like that would happen again. Not if she had anything to do with it.

The commissioner arrived. As before, he was ushered to his table by a smiling hostess. Once again, he found Mr. Porcini there waiting for him. A waiter appeared, delivering a platter of appetizers, the kind the commissioner had enjoyed before. It was almost as if the scene were repeating itself, as if a tape had been rewound, though now there would be a new ending, a happy ending, they'd all be given a second chance. Mr. Porcini leaned back a bit in his chair and smiled.

The commissioner enjoyed a tasty lunch. On the advice of Porcini, he ordered tuna steak, which was served on a bed of colorful summer vegetables cut into delicate julienne strips. He topped off the meal with a small but brisk cup of espresso coffee, which he sipped between bites of a custardy pear tart served with a refreshing scoop of lemon gelato. After which he, too, leaned back in his chair. He patted his stomach, satisfied.

"So," he said. "I suppose you are wondering about your lease. Whether or not we will renew it next year."

"Yes, yes," Mr. Porcini said eagerly.

"Well, I think we can all agree," said the commissioner, "that Fare in the Square is certainly an asset to the park, despite the unfortunate trouble you had here on my last visit. I was informed by my park manager, Celia Fuentes, that that was a problem created when the children had to abandon the playgrounds. You know my park manager Celia, of course. I'm sure she's been of help to you."

"Celia . . ." Mr. Porcini tried to place her. He wasn't sure who she was. "Of course," he answered quickly. "Wonderful woman. Most helpful."

"It's unfortunate about the playgrounds," said the commissioner. "Though the problem there seems to have resolved itself. As mysteriously as it arose."

The two men glanced up at the playground nearby. The sounds of children playing happily, without accident—and at a very pleasant distance, both were thinking—filled the air.

"So," said Commissioner Greene, "after much thought, and after studying the many benefits that Fare in the Square has brought to Union Square, I know you will be happy to hear that we have decided to—"

Mr. Porcini sat on the edge of his seat, nodding, grinning, leaning forward to hear the answer he had been waiting for. Instead, he heard a whistle. For at that moment, Hiram had pulled out the whistle that had served him so well the night before. Hiram had been hiding behind the fountain that tinkled merrily in the center of the restaurant. Now he emerged to blow the whistle loudly. And shrilly. At which signal the rats, all the many rats who had hidden themselves so carefully the night before, jumped out. And ran around the restaurant harum-scarum.

The chaos that ensued! People screamed. People leaped from their chairs. People ran hither and thither. But there was no escaping the rats. Rats were everywhere. They ran over people's shoes. They jumped onto tables and chairs. Eek! People shrieked, terrified. So terrified that they failed to notice the elf, who by now had climbed to the top of the fountain and stood there, hanging by one hand, laughing, waving his free arm, urging the rats on. And no one noticed that it was his signal, one final blow of his whistle, that caused the rats to scatter again, to run from the restaurant and back through the park, into the safety of their holes.

The commissioner pushed back his chair and made fast to leave.

"Commissioner!" cried Mr. Porcini. "I can explain everything!"

But the commissioner was already striding toward the gate. Mr. Porcini chased after him.

"This restaurant isn't the problem!" he cried. "You know who the culprit is? The Greenmarket! I'm telling you! They're the ones who attract rodents!"

He leaped over a chair to catch up.

"This morning—Ben, listen!—my staff found produce all over. Greenmarket produce! I run a clean establishment! Pristine!"

By this time, the commissioner was climbing the stairs, taking them two at a time. He stopped only long enough to say this:

"Porcini, I came here to deliver good news. But I'm afraid I must reconsider my decision. Right now I must go back to my office. And determine the best way to proceed."

At the far end of the restaurant, similarly shaken, Will sat at a table, the table he'd taken to frequenting, his notebook still trembling in his hand. Had he just seen what he thought he'd seen? Had enough rats to populate a pirate ship just jumped out, as if on cue, and chased willy-nilly around the restaurant? Perhaps it was just a dream. More like a night-mare. But it *had* happened, and Will had a story, a story if ever there was one.

Could he write it? No one would believe it. No one would believe that hundreds of rats—no, it must've been thousands—had swelled like a swarm, then disappeared just as quickly. But where?

Somewhere into the Square . . .

13 ALERT THE MEDIA!

It did not take long for the people of Union Square to hear about the rats. News of that sort travels fast. Though the people who heard the news thought it sounded so horrendous, so outlandish, they weren't really sure it could be true. Rats? By the hundreds? Maybe thousands? Running harum-scarum through Union Square? It had to be a rumor, some sort of crazy rumor.

Now, as everyone who lives in New York knows, rumors of this sort have circulated through the city before. Rumors about terrible things, outrageous things, things that turned out, in the end, not to be true at all. The most famous of these was the rumor about the alligators. Alligators? In New York City? The story, as it was told over the years by one New Yorker to another, went something like this:

A while ago, some families from New York City traveled to Florida for vacation, and when they returned, they brought home souvenirs. Live souvenirs. Tiny baby alligators farmed in the Florida swamps. The alligators were cute enough when they were little, but when they started growing, the families realized they could no longer keep them in their New York City apartments. Not knowing what else to do with the wriggling—soon to be raging—reptiles, they flushed the little lizards down their toilets.

Oh, but the alligators didn't die, or so the story went. They took up residence in the sewers, where they swam around quite happily and had babies of their own. And where soon their population was thriving. Which meant that there were now alligators—whole colonies of them—living in the New York City sewers.

Of course, anyone who heard this rumor was bound to become worried. People worried that the alligators would swim through the sewers and poke their heads right back up through the toilets. Which would leave anyone sitting on one (and, of course, their bare bottoms) more than a little exposed.

After a time, though, the people of New York City figured out that the alligator story was just that. A story. A myth, an urban legend that sprouted up in the concrete city much like a plucky weed might push up through a crack in a sidewalk. And so, when people now heard the rat story, it sounded suspiciously similar. It seemed to them like something that was just as unlikely to have actually happened, a story designed merely to scare them. Another rumor, nothing more.

Which is why people were more than a little surprised when an article about the rats appeared in the paper the next morning, an article written by William Manley, who claimed to have seen the rats with his own two unbiased and reportorial eyes.

Oh, dear, people fretted. If *The New York Times* said that rats had overrun the park, it must be true.

Still, it confused people that the park didn't really appear to be any different. It was quiet, certainly, quieter than usual, since many of the people who had heard the story stayed out of the park *just in case* it might be true. But the quiet itself seemed to confirm that nothing was wrong. If all those rats had been running around the park, where were they now? Surely they wouldn't *all* have gone back undercover. Surely at least a few would still be running about, terrorizing the good citizens of Union Square. . . .

A short way from the park, holed up in their apartment, Jack and Mimi had not heard about the rats. Neither of them had gone outside that day, so they hadn't yet bought a copy of the paper. Jack and Mimi had spent the morning at home, where Jack had busied himself drawing sketches of the soap suspect. Sketches, at least, of how Jack imagined he might look. Of course, there'd been no eyewitnesses, no one to confirm that the man in question had hollow eyes, a bushy mustache, and fleshy jowls. But Jack had worked through the morning, drawing sketch after sketch, refining the features until he'd arrived at a portrait of a very suspicious-looking man.

And now that Jack had a sketch, he reasoned, he could continue his search in earnest.

"Mom," said Jack, flashing the portrait before her. "What do you think?"

"Mmm," said Mimi distractedly.

"It's the culprit," Jack explained. "I finally got it. This is what he looks like."

Mimi frowned. That morning she'd felt drawn into one too many conversations about the so-called culprit.

"Enough with the detective nonsense," she snapped irritably. Though immediately she felt sorry she'd said it.

"I'm sorry," she said quickly. "Don't pay any attention to me. Obviously, I'm in a bad mood."

"So how about we go out?" said Jack.

Mimi eyed him. "Both of us?" she asked suspiciously. "Why? To look for the culprit?"

"Yeah, and to set up the lemonade stand."

"Oh. So you need me to lug the lemonade supplies."

"Which will end up being good for you as well as me."

Mimi eyed Jack skeptically.

"The lemonade stand will give me the perfect cover for being in the park," said Jack. "Plus, it'll bring me that much closer to getting Avenger's Revenge."

"But you said it would be good for *me*."

"It will. 'Cause if I was busy with Avenger's Revenge, I wouldn't be bothering you with any more of my detective nonsense, would I?"

Mimi laughed in spite of herself.

Thinking. Jack was always thinking. How could she say no? The two of them set about bundling up the supplies.

But when Jack and Mimi arrived in the park, they were surprised to see the place looking so empty.

At the far edge of the park, a few other people were gathering. These were people who'd heard about the rats, and who'd come because they were curious, or because they found comfort in times of uncertainty in banding with their fellows. When they saw Jack there, his stand set bravely near the fence guarding the center lawn, his face young and hopeful, they felt brave enough themselves to venture farther into the park. They drifted toward Jack, their newspapers clutched to their bosoms, and soon the boy was surrounded by a knot of people, all buying lemonade, all more than happy to tell Jack and his mom what they had read in *The Times,* what terrible thing had happened in the park the day before, or at least what terrible thing had been reported.

As the people stood there, talking and sipping their lemonades, they looked around the park a bit warily. They looked across the walkways, now nearly abandoned. They looked into the center lawn, which was locked, as it had been for weeks now. The center lawn where once they'd sunned. And sprawled. And smooched . . .

The people in the park wondered: Where had all the rats gone?

And the scarier question: Would they return?

In another part of the park, another group arrived— Ginger and the members of MADAT. Their children— Christopher and Christie among them—were busy making signs, hand-lettering them with messages like WE WANT A SAF PARC! And RATS AR NOT HELTHY FOUR CHELDRN! Their parents tore off pieces of duct tape and taped the signs onto sticks.

Not far from this group stood Will. He'd returned to the park to talk to Celia. And now he was interviewing her, or trying to. Though he was having trouble getting Celia to cooperate.

"Did you see the rats?" he asked her.

"No," she answered curtly.

"You didn't?" he pressed.

"Not exactly."

Celia bit her lip. *Dios mío!* What had she just admitted to this reporter? Because of the rats, she was already deep in trouble with her boss. And now the reporter was trying to drag her in deeper? She hoped it wouldn't cost her her job.

Just then, a limousine pulled up to the park. Now, it should be noted that a limousine, in and of itself, was not an unusual sight around Union Square. People frequently arrived by limo to eat at any of the fashionable restaurants that had sprung up in the neighborhood in recent years.

But this limousine didn't pull up to any of the restaurants. It pulled directly into the parking lot of the Square, where it wedged itself between two farm trucks, there selling produce at the Greenmarket.

The windows of the limousine were tinted darkly. The people in the park strained to see who would emerge.

The door swung open. Two men stepped out. One was Benjamin Greene, the parks commissioner. The other was Bernie Stern, the mayor of New York City. And with him came the usual trail of aides and assistants who always accompanied the mayor.

The people in the park turned to each other, concerned. The mayor! With the parks commissioner! Their arrival could only confirm the story they'd heard, the disturbing rumor about the rats. Why else would these two pull up together in their slick City Hall limousine?

"Mayor Stern!" cried Will. He ran toward the limo. "Do you have any comment about the rats?"

The mayor's face remained inscrutable, as fixed and immobile as a mask. "I have come to investigate the situation," he said.

Mayor Stern, Commissioner Greene, and their entourage moved as one into the park, looking not unlike a giant spider with a mess of unruly legs. Commissioner Greene pointed. To the Greenmarket. To Fare in the Square. Mayor Stern nodded. He looked stern. More so even than he usually looked, and that was quite stern indeed.

As he passed Jack's lemonade stand, the mayor held out his hand. Jack handed him a cup of lemonade. The mayor drank it down in one quick gulp and held out his cup for a refill, though, as Jack noticed, he hadn't yet paid for the first. His eyes were scanning the park.

Jack refilled the mayor's cup. The mayor drank it. The mayor's aide, looking concerned, whispered something in the mayor's ear. It was then that Mayor Stern finally turned and looked at Jack. He seemed surprised to see him—a boy, so young, just a boy—manning the stand. He set down the cup and walked away quickly, without so much as a thank you, much less the dollar he owed as payment.

The mayor and his entourage headed to the statue of Abraham Lincoln. There, as if by magic, a gathering of reporters had appeared. Photographers from the daily papers.

TV reporters clutching their microphones and shouldering their cameras.

Someone had alerted the media.

The mayor hushed the crowd.

"In response to recent events in Union Square," he announced, "we have made the decision to close the Greenmarket. And the restaurant, as well, Fare in the Square."

"Fare in the Square?" shouted a voice. It was Mr. Porcini. "No!"

"The two will be shuttered," said the mayor, "for the health and safety of the citizens of this great city."

"For how long?" a reporter shouted out.

"Until further notice," said the mayor.

The reporters shouted out other questions, but the mayor didn't answer. He pushed back through the crowd, the people parting around him, stunned. Mr. Porcini slumped onto a bench, Giovanni beside him. In the Greenmarket the farmers began slowly, resignedly, to pack their produce back into its crates to bring it back to their farms.

The mayor and his staff piled into their limousine. But before they left, the aide who had earlier whispered something in the mayor's ear now approached Officer DeShields and whispered something in hers. And as he did so, he pointed to Jack.

As the limousine backed out from between the two farm trucks and angled out of the park, Officer DeShields swaggered up to Jack.

"Orders are," she said gruffly, "you've got to take down this lemonade stand. I'm talking now."

"Take down the stand?" said Jack. "Why?"

"Vending without a license," said Officer DeShields. "You got a license?"

Jack shook his head.

"I didn't think so. Look," said Officer DeShields. "I'll level with you. Personally? I'm not against lemonade stands. I had one myself when I was a kid. But if you're gonna sell food in the park, you gotta have a license. And after what happened here yesterday, you can bet the mayor wants to make sure there's nothing in this place that's gonna attract more rats. So take down the stand, kid. And let's move on."

Mimi, who had been standing, stunned, with the others, suddenly noticed that a policewoman was talking to her son. She rushed over to see what was wrong.

"Officer DeShields," she said, glancing at the name on her badge. "I'm sorry. We didn't realize. Of course we'll take down the stand."

Will, too, hurried over.

"What seems to be the problem?" he asked.

"There's no problem," said Officer DeShields. "No problem at all. As long as this kid clears outta here with his lemonade stand."

"But it's only a lemonade stand," argued Will. "What harm can it do?"

"He's breaking the law," she said.

Will stood there a moment, considering. It was true that Jack was breaking the law. He'd suspected that from the start. Still. Jack was just a kid. A kid with a lemonade stand . . .

Will didn't know why, exactly, but he felt agitated that

Jack had to abandon the stand. And he didn't know what made him say what he said next, or how the words even came to him, but he heard himself saying this:

"Officer, this boy is my child, my sole surviving child, the rest we lost to a tragic accident, having to do with a camping trip. And a grizzly. Recently, I lost my job, and my wife here got fired from hers. So the family's been counting on our enterprising young Jack to provide a small trickle of income."

Jack stared at Will. In awe. This guy was funny! Mimi stared, too. In horror and disbelief.

"The income from the stand gives us just enough to buy a crust of bread," Will went on. "Stale, certainly. But enough to sustain us."

Officer DeShields narrowed her eyes. "So," she said. "You're a wise guy, eh? I'll tell you what. Maybe this'll help with the family finances. How about a summons? One that'll translate into a hundred-dollar fine, easy. I wasn't going to hit the kid with a summons, but now that his father's being a first-class jerk, I think it's the only thing to do."

"Officer!" cried Mimi. "This man isn't my husband!"

Officer DeShields tossed her a skeptical look.

"He's not!" Mimi insisted. "I don't know why he's saying this. He isn't the boy's father!"

"Oh, no?" said Officer DeShields as she wrote out the summons and handed it to Jack. "So who is? The Easter Bunny?"

Jack didn't remember much of what was said after that. Mimi wheeled toward Will and started shouting. Will was quick to shout back. All the shouting hurt Jack's ears. He dropped to the ground to escape the sound.

But as Jack sat down, he came face-to-face with someone, someone he had been hoping to meet, had pictured, even. Though the face he saw did not have hollow eyes, a bushy mustache, or fleshy jowls. It was a small face, remarkably small, a face unlike any Jack had ever seen before. And that face belonged to Hiram, who'd been drawn to the scene and stayed there too long in order to savor the skirmish.

Jack was so surprised to see an elf staring him in the face—an elf!—that he was struck speechless. His mouth fell open, though not a word came out.

Hiram didn't budge—as he should have. He didn't run, he didn't hide. He just stood there, staring Jack in the eye, with a grin that looked not-a-little nasty smeared across his sour, weather-beaten face.

Jack tugged on his mother's sleeve. "Mom," he managed to say.

But Mimi didn't hear him. She was still yelling at Will.

"Mom!" Jack said more insistently.

Mimi whirled around. "What is it?" she snapped. Jack pointed to the space beside him.

"An elf . . ." he murmured.

Though by that time, there was no one there.

Hiram had disappeared.

14 ENOUGH IS ENOUGH!

Mimi didn't hear what Jack had said. And neither did anyone else in the park. Because at that moment in Union Square, something else was happening. Something big. Something that had been simmering in the park for a long while finally bubbled up to a boil. For there is only so much that people can take, and in the past weeks, the people of Union Square had withstood quite a lot.

There'd been the dog poop, of course. That had been up-setting enough. But that had been followed—and so quickly!—by that spate of unexplained accidents. After which, children had overrun the restaurant, upsetting more than a few trays.

And after that, there'd been the rats.

The rats . . .

All this had made the people of Union Square jumpy. And that morning, when they'd arrived in the park, they'd been the jumpiest yet. When they had seen the mayor pull up, they'd felt a surge of hope. Maybe he would calm their fears. But he hadn't, had he? If anything, he'd made them worse. When he'd closed down the Greenmarket and the restau-rant, he'd done so so abruptly, and with so little explanation, really, that the people of Union Square found themselves more worried than ever. And with a long string of unanswered questions.

After the mayor had left and Officer DeShields had slapped Jack with a summons . . . Oh, yes, the people in the park had seen *that*. They'd watched the policewoman stride up to Jack. Jack, that sweet young boy with the lemonade stand. They'd watched her saddle him with a summons, a summons that would cost his hardworking mother—a teacher, wasn't she?—a hundred dollars. *A hundred dollars!* For something as innocent as a *lemonade stand????*

It was then that something in them snapped.

"Enough is enough!" someone shouted.

As fate would have it, at that moment, a woman happened through the market walking her newly groomed poodle.

"Come along, Foo Foo," she said.

She paraded the dog past the egg stand, where a farmer was busy packing his eggs back into their crates. Someone— it is impossible to know who exactly, since everything happened so fast—grabbed an egg and hurled it—*splat!*— directly at the very surprised little Foo Foo.

"Enough is enough!" the person shouted.

Someone else grabbed an egg. And another person after that. Soon, a whole host of people were hurling eggs at the hapless pooch and the unfortunate woman who walked him.

The woman covered her head. She ran, pulling Foo Foo toward the dog run, where she hoped to find safety. But the mob of people followed, pelting them not only with eggs now, but with anything else they could grab as they ran through the market. Tomatoes (vine-ripened). Peaches (organic). Muffins (sugar-free). Even pies! The woman slammed the gate of the dog run behind her. How could she defend herself? She ran to the waste can and pulled out some poop.

"Enough is enough!" she shouted, hurling it back over the fence.

There were other people at the dog run, and when they saw what was happening, they were quick to jump to their comrade's aid. They, too, grabbed up handfuls of poop and fired it over the fence, trying to stave back the mob.

The mob stormed the gate. The gate crashed open. The dogs who'd been in the run, yelping and yipping, now escaped, running frightened into the crowd.

Oh, what a free-for-all Union Square had become. Fights were erupting all over the park. At the market, scores more grabbed up produce. The farmers had protested—at first. But soon they, too, were grabbing up ammo—one potato, two potatoes, three potatoes, four!—and chucking it into the crowd.

Something hit Celia, something hard. A potato? No! It was a broom! Celia turned to see who'd thrown it.

It was a park worker! One of her own! Sleep-deprived and seething. *All those mornings at 6:00 A.M. . . .*

"Enough is enough!" he shouted.

Celia grabbed up the broom and aimed it back, but the fellow disappeared from sight, swallowed back up by the crowd.

Ah, but Celia's eye happened on someone else, someone against whom she'd long been nursing her own bitter grudge. It was Mr. Porcini, cowering on a bench with Giovanni, the two of them gaping in disbelief at the ruckus roiling all around.

The sight of Mr. Porcini, plump as a mushroom, his face gray and spongy, made Celia even angrier. Enough was enough! She hurled the broom at him. It whistled through the air like a spear.

Mr. Porcini ducked. The broom sailed past, grazing Giovanni on the shoulder.

"Who in the world . . . ?" Mr. Porcini stammered.

Giovanni rubbed his shoulder. "I think her name is to be Celia," he said.

"Celia?" said Mr. Porcini.

"The one who head up the park."

Celia grabbed what was nearest at hand, a gooey blue-berry pie.

"Eat this, you moldy toadstool!" she shouted. "Who cares about your stupid tapenade!"

"Tapenade?" Mr. Porcini spluttered.

Fwop! The pie struck him in the face.

Giovanni jumped up. He started to chase after Celia, but something—no, it was someone—slammed into him.

Christopher! The twin had taken advantage of the chaos erupting around him to break free of MADAT. He'd run off willy-nilly, knocking straight into Giovanni—*oof!*—with his sign.

"You!" Giovanni shouted. He yanked the sign from Christopher. With his bare hands Giovanni ripped the card-board to pieces.

RATS, WANT, PARC, the pieces now said.

Christopher grabbed the stick. Giovanni yanked back. The two of them pulled, this way and that, in an angry, stubborn tug-of-war.

"Yahoo!" The victory was Christopher's! He charged triumphantly back through the crowd, raising the stick high, like a sword.

Not far away, Christopher's mother, Ginger, was completely unaware that her son had bolted from her, that he'd been engaged in a fierce tug-of-war, or that he now brandished a jagged, pointy stick through the crowd. Ginger's eyes were elsewhere. On the lawn, the center lawn. Fenced off, as it had been for so long now, its gates secured with a lock.

The lawn! Why hadn't she thought of it before? It suddenly occurred to Ginger that the lawn would be the perfect place for the new playground she'd envisioned! Much bigger than the dog run! And so much more central than the restaurant! The lawn, rolling and expansive, sitting smack in the center of the Square—the lawn was clearly the prize!

Ginger picked up her megaphone. "MADAT!" she shouted. "Attention, all members of MADAT! You see that lawn? That huge, green lawn? Imagine it filled with swings! And with slides! Imagine pools of water there! And your children, happily splashing!"

"The lawn . . . ," people murmured.

"Take the lawn!" cried Ginger. "Take it now! Claim the lawn as ours!"

One of the mothers, the one with the long, fuzzy braid, stared at Ginger, appalled. The center lawn for a playground?

But the lawn was for everyone—not only for toddlers who wanted to run, but for grown-ups who wanted to read. For workers who wanted to lunch. And sweethearts who snuggled in the grass. If the lawn were a playground, where would all those other people go? How pushy, how greedy, could one person be?

Face time? she thought. She'd wised up quite a bit about face time.

She grabbed a roll of duct tape, tape she'd earlier been using to fasten sticks to signs, and ripped off a piece—a large piece, for that was obviously what was required—and slapped it over Ginger's mouth.

"Mmm!" protested Ginger. "Mmm! Mmm!"

"Enough is enough!" shouted the woman.

But though she succeeded in silencing Ginger, she could not distract the crowd. It was too late for that. When Ginger had called attention to the lawn, people had heard her. They'd looked from the grass to the fence that guarded it. And a hunger for the grass, that soft, supple grass, had gnawed, suddenly, at their insides.

"The lawn!" someone shouted.

That person jumped the fence. Others followed quickly. Soon, everyone was leaping onto the lawn.

"No!" shouted Celia, running up, trying to stop them. "Not my lawn!"

Someone elbowed Celia, pushing her out of the way. Another person knocked her down. As people stampeded past, scrambling to climb the fence, Celia was nearly trampled.

Officer DeShields rushed over and helped Celia to her feet. She radioed for help as around them people fought and shouted. As they threw things and kicked each other. As they punched. . . .

All the passions in the park had finally come to blows.

A few feet from the lawn, Lincoln regarded the riot, his eyes widening. He felt stirred and excited by the sight of so many people in the Square pitched in so heated a battle. Wouldn't he like to join in?

He would!

Lincoln made a move to head for the lawn, where the battle was thickest, the brawl abroil, but when he tried to walk, he was surprised to find that his feet refused to cooperate. He couldn't get them, somehow, to separate. As he took a step, his legs buckled underneath him, and the poor man went sprawling.

What in the . . . ?

Lincoln looked down at his feet.

His shoelaces were tied together!

Why, that no-good, stinking, miserable little elf!

Lincoln undid his shoelaces and scrambled to his feet. He clenched his fist and shouted into the air.

"Show your face, you wretched runt!"

"Here I am," taunted a voice near his ear.

Lincoln whipped toward the sound. The elf was on his shoulder! Perched within reach!

Lincoln grabbed, though not quickly enough. His hands closed only on air.

"All right," he cried. "Where'd you go? Where'd you go?"

Something tickled his tummy. A ridge ruffled his shirt. Hiram's head popped out from between the buttons.

"Try and catch me," Hiram teased.

Lincoln slapped at his chest, but the elf's head was gone. He felt something crawling down his pant leg—inching like a caterpillar, pinching like a crab. The elf burst out at the foot.

"Missed me!" brayed Hiram.

"Why, you little—"

But then, just as quickly, Hiram disappeared again, only to pop, a moment later, out of a pocket, one of the side pockets in Lincoln's pants.

Lincoln lunged. Aha! This time, he caught the elf! He seized him by the throat.

Lincoln smiled, savoring the moment. This was, after all, a moment he'd been waiting for for a long time. He stroked the elf's throat, leering with satisfaction. Such a *tiny* throat. Such a *vulnerable* little throat. Why, it was no bigger around, really, than the neck of a chicken. Which could snap . . .

Ouch! Hiram bit Lincoln, hard, very hard, and as Lincoln shook his smarting fingers, Hiram scrambled free. This time, when Lincoln grabbed for him, he didn't catch him. All he managed to snag was his hat. The elf's dirty little hat. As grungy and nasty as the scoundrel who'd worn it.

Elsewhere in the park, someone else was grappling. Though not with an elf. Officer DeShields was grappling with her conscience, her sense of what she, an officer sworn to uphold the law, should be doing during this riot. She'd shouted herself hoarse trying to be heard over the melee. Should she rush the center lawn and try to stem the chaos that had erupted there? But how could she? She was just one lone police officer against a tide of violence. How could she be expected to bring order when so many were so far out of control?

Officer DeShields took off her cap and glanced at the angel pasted there. A picture, nothing more than a picture. No help at all. She looked around anxiously. Where were the other officers she'd called? How long would it take them to come to her aid?

Officer DeShields clapped on her cap. She knew she had to act. She had to do something, however small, to bring order to the disorder in the park. Perhaps she could go after one person. Yes. That was a good idea. Someone at the edge of the crowd, perhaps.

And that's when she spotted Lincoln.

Lincoln. Who was dancing around and shrieking loudly. Lincoln. Who seemed to be slapping at himself. She'd seen the man act strangely before, but this took the cake. What in the world was he doing now?

By the time Officer DeShields reached Lincoln, he had quieted. He was standing still, clutching Hiram's filthy hat forlornly in his hand.

"What's going on here?" Officer DeShields demanded.

"He got away," Lincoln whimpered. "I let him get away."

"Let me see your identification," Officer DeShields demanded.

Identification? Lincoln blinked at her, hard, as if the offi-

cer had flashed a blinding light in his eyes. He had no identification card, she must know that. Why, he was lucky, day
to day, if he could scrape together a buck in change for a cup
of coffee and a day-old doughnut, how was he supposed to
come by an ID?

"Charmayne," he said. Her name dripped off his tongue
like honey off a spoon.

Officer DeShields started. Lincoln knew her name? How
did he find out that?

"Charmayne," Lincoln cooed again. "My little sugar plum."
He smacked his lips suggestively.

Officer DeShields lurched back.

"ID," she insisted crisply.

Lincoln grumbled. He crammed Hiram's hat into the
pocket of his pants, and, to satisfy her, rummaged around
there as if looking for identification. As he fished, he felt
something, something other than the hat, something stuffed
farther down. Something smooth. And slippery. Lincoln
pulled it out. What in the world . . . ?

It was a bar of soap.

"Soap?" Lincoln wondered aloud. "How'd I get a bar of
soap?"

Officer DeShields stared at the bar Lincoln held in his
hands. She remembered what Ginger had told her when
she'd warned her about Lincoln and the playgrounds. It had
involved a bar of soap, hadn't it?

"What have you got there?" she asked warily.

"Dunno," said Lincoln. "The elf must've put it there. He
must've put soap in my pocket."

"Hand it over," demanded Officer DeShields.

Lincoln grinned. So the officer wanted something, did she? Something he actually had? Well, he didn't have to give it to her, did he?

"Try and make me," he said.

He closed his fist around the bar and pitched it into the crowd.

Officer DeShields felt her pulse quicken. Lincoln was proving more difficult than she had expected. He was unruly, just as unruly as the crowds. When she spoke, her voice shook, betraying just how jangled she felt.

"Destroying evidence, are you?" she said. "Resisting an officer of the law?"

Enough was enough.

Just then, sirens screamed up to the Square, the sirens of all the many police cars she'd summoned to help her. Officer DeShields imagined how the Square must look to those who were just arriving. Wild. Lawless. Completely out of control. Which reflected badly on her, of course, the fact that things on her beat had come to such a pass. It would look as if she'd allowed it. And things would look better, she knew, if she'd been able to arrest at least one person, if she'd been able to get even one of the troublemakers in handcuffs and under control.

"You're under arrest," she announced to Lincoln.

Lincoln looked longingly at the battlefield, the battlefield where he'd been headed before the elf had tripped him. Before he'd been detained by an officer of the law. He felt something cold clamp onto his wrists. Officer DeShields was tugging at him, at the handcuffs that now shackled him. She was leading him away.

"No!" Lincoln shouted loudly. "Not with the Union in peril!"

The police who'd arrived jumped out of their cars, their billy clubs drawn and at the ready. They rushed the lawn, driving back the mob, and as they charged, the people scattered. People shot across the grass. They hurdled back over the fence. People screeched and screamed, fleeing the park altogether.

Until all that was left was a lawn full of poop.

And smashed fruits and vegetables, rotting in the sun.

And some pieces of broken-up signs.

The lawn cleared, their job accomplished, the police swaggered back to their cars. Only Celia remained. She stood at the edge of the lawn, her lawn, now trampled beyond recognition. She looked at the fence, her fence, once so beautiful, now mown down, bulldozed, so heartlessly, by the hordes.

Celia would have to alert Commissioner Greene about this. She'd have to tell him what happened.

And what would the commissioner say now?

As Celia slunk off to make the call, Hiram shinned down the flagpole. He smiled at the debris and destruction stretching out before him.

His lawn now looked exactly the way he liked it.

Plenty of refuse and rubbish.

All that garbage littering up the place.

And not a single person in sight.

15 Caution: Rodenticide!

The next day, the people who lived around Union Square woke up feeling bad. Perhaps, after you've had a fight, you've noticed this happen yourself. Maybe you said something mean to someone, or yelled at someone, a friend, maybe, or someone in your family. And maybe, at the time you were doing it, it felt good. Satisfying, even. But after a while, you may have found yourself feeling bad that you yelled at the person or said something nasty. You might even have found that it made you feel a lot worse, not better.

And so it was that morning as the sun broke over Union Square. As the people in the neighborhood opened their eyes, they didn't like what they saw. Images of themselves. Acting badly.

Did I really throw an egg at that poodle? they wondered. Was that really me who elbowed and shoved, just to trample over some fence?

How had any of this happened?

One thing was certain. People did not feel very proud of themselves. Some clapped their pillows back over their heads and tried to get back to sleep. But the clocks by their bed-sides ticked away insistently. And eventually, people knew they had to rouse themselves. Though they did so with very little spirit. They ate their breakfasts silently, sullenly. They dressed themselves without caring, putting on old, dirty shirts and soiled socks. And when they trudged out of their apartments and down the street, they trained their eyes on their shoes, not meeting the glance of a single person they passed.

Not far from the Square, Mimi sat at her kitchen table, sipping her morning cup of tea. Her cat curled around her ankles, but Mimi nudged him away. She didn't feel like petting Bullseye. Not this morning. She'd woken up with a headache, no doubt caused by all that yelling she'd done the day before. She cupped her forehead in her hands as she remembered what she'd said.

Had she really called that reporter a lunkhead and a peabrain? Had she actually told him she thought his name should be *Juvenile*, not *Manley*?

Eeeesh! She poured herself another cup of tea, and got up to add more milk.

Oh, no. There wasn't any milk. Not a single drop left in the carton.

"Jack," Mimi called irritably. "Did you just finish the milk?"

In his room, Jack took another bite of cereal. "Maybe," he called back.

"And you put the empty carton back in the refrigerator?" No answer.

"Well, I have to run across the street. To the deli. I'll be gone five minutes, nothing more."

In his room, Jack smiled. He'd been waiting for just such an opportunity. When Mimi locked the door behind her, he dug out the phone book from under her desk and paged through. He had to find a number. The number of *The New York Times*. When he found it, he picked up the phone and dialed.

"William Manley, please," he said when the receptionist answered.

The receptionist transferred him to Will's line.

"Will," said Jack when he answered. "It's me. Jack. I have to tell you something."

Will was glad to hear Jack's voice. He'd been wanting to call Jack himself. And also Mimi, of course. He'd been sitting at his desk, wanting to apologize, feeling terrible about what he'd done. He remembered in particular what Mimi had said about his name. Actually, if he had to admit it, what she'd said was all too true.

And funny. Oh, yes, funny. So Mimi had a sense of humor after all.

"Jack," he said. "I'm glad you called. But actually, I'm just about to run out. I'm going downtown to interview Lincoln. Did you know he got arrested yesterday?"

"Well," said Jack, "what I called to tell you sort of relates to Lincoln. Kind of." He hesitated. Could he tell Will? He might as well just blurt it out. "I'm calling you because I found out who's been causing all the trouble in the park."

"You think it's Lincoln?"

"No," said Jack. "Not Lincoln. I don't think you're going to believe it."

"Try me."

"Well," Jack started. There was a long pause as he thought about how he would say what he had to say. "Remember the clues? Remember the nannies said it was a mischievous spirit? But then we found the soap and figured it was a person?"

"I'm with you so far," said Will.

"Well, it's not a spirit. But it's not exactly a person, either. More like something in between."

"What are you talking about?" said Will.

"It's an elf," Jack blurted out.

"An elf?"

"The one Lincoln's always talking about. I saw him with my own two eyes. While you and Mom were arguing. I sat down on the ground and came face-to-face with him. The elf, I mean. He has a really nasty scowl."

Will wasn't sure how to respond. For a moment there, he had thought Jack might be about to give him some information, real information that might lead to the culprit. What had he been thinking? Jack was a kid, not a colleague. A nice kid, but one with an active imagination apparently. Will shuffled some papers around his desk as he considered what he might say.

"Are you writing down what I'm telling you?" asked Jack.

"Sure," Will said quickly. "Sure I am." He grabbed a piece of paper and scribbled down some notes. He didn't want to hurt Jack's feelings. Might as well let him think he believed him. Maybe he should even ask him a few questions.

"Okay," said Will. "Tell me this. What exactly did this elf look like?"

"He was old," said Jack. "Really old."

"How could you tell?" asked Will.

"His face was all wrinkled. You know, weathered."

Will thought back to the elves he had read about when he was a boy.

"Did he wear a pointy hat?" asked Will. "And a bright green suit with striped socks?"

"No way!" cried Jack. "He was dressed all in brown. Well, brown and green, I think, but the green was *dark* green. *Camouflage* colors. So he could blend right in with the park. He did have a hat, but that was camouflage, too. It had a dirty little tassel at the end."

"Hmm," said Will, to humor Jack. "Camouflage. That would explain why no one's ever seen him before, wouldn't it?"

"Except Lincoln," Jack reminded him. "Lincoln's seen him."

"True enough."

"It all made sense when I saw him," said Jack. "I mean, he must be the one causing all the terrible things in the park lately. Nothing else could explain it. Nobody else could be so mean."

Will wrote down what Jack said. He was still writing when Jack added this: "We could use the spirit of Gandhi here, know what I mean? Now more than ever."

Will stopped writing midword. What an odd thing for a kid to say. So adult, really. So thoughtful.

"Why do you say that?" Will asked.

"Well, everybody's been fighting so much lately, you know? I mean, fighting a little is one thing, but yesterday was scary. To see everybody fighting so much."

"I know what you mean," said Will.

"It got me wondering. Why do people fight like that, anyway?"

"Maybe they think they're right," said Will, remembering his own part in the melee. "Maybe they're convinced that the other guy's the bad guy, the other guy's gotta be the one who's wrong."

"Maybe the bad guy is really *us*," said Jack. "I mean, something running wild inside us. You know, inside our hearts."

Will whistled, long and slow. This kid was a regular font of wisdom. "How'd you come up with that?" he asked.

"I didn't," Jack admitted. "Not exactly. I mean, my mom said it."

"Your mom?"

"Well, not my mom exactly, either," said Jack. "Gandhi said it. Or at least he said something like it. My mom was the one who told me."

"Your mom's been quoting Gandhi?" said Will. He smiled at the thought. "I'm impressed."

"She doesn't always yell," Jack said sheepishly. "And anyway, I'm not so sure about what she said. It doesn't make sense completely. Because there *is* a bad guy out there. And he's *not* just inside us. It's the elf. I saw him with my own two eyes."

Just then, Jack heard Mimi's key in the door.

"Uh-oh," he whispered. "Gotta go."

"Can I talk to your mom?" asked Will. This was his chance, his chance to apologize.

"No!" hissed Jack. "I'll talk to you later. But hey," he said before he hung up, "when you see Lincoln? Ask him about the elf. I bet he has a lot more to say about him than me."

As Jack predicted, Lincoln did have a lot to say. Though it was not exactly the sort of information Will had expected. When Will walked up to the jail cell where Lincoln was being held, Lincoln kicked at the bars between them.

"Hello, Lincoln," Will introduced himself. "I'm Will Manley, a reporter for *The New York Times*. I heard you got arrested yesterday. Can you tell me a little about what happened?"

"Why don't *you* tell *me*?" said Lincoln, turning the tables. "You're Mr. Big Reporter Answerman, am I right? How about *I* ask *you* a question?"

Will started. It looked as if Lincoln was going to be a tough interview. "Yeah?" he asked hesitantly.

"What's smaller than a breadbox and fits into my pocket?"

Lincoln was staring at him, expecting an answer.

"I don't know," Will stumbled. "A, um . . . handkerchief?"

"Soap."

Soap? What did Lincoln know about soap?

"So the elf thinks I'm dirty, does he?" Lincoln railed. "Well, I got news for him. *He's* the one's dirty!"

"Wait a minute. Wait a minute," said Will. "What are you saying here? You have soap?"

"Had," said Lincoln, chuckling.

"Where's it now?" asked Will.

"That police lady tried to get it from me. Cha-a-a-r-ma-a-ayne," he drawled. "But I foiled her. I threw it into the crowd."

"Okay," suggested Will. "Let's start at the beginning here. You say you had soap? In your pocket?"

"The elf put it there."

"And the policewoman tried to get it from you? Slow down and tell me the whole story."

Lincoln tugged at his beard, as if the thought upset him.

"In your own words," prompted Will.

"In my own words?" Lincoln's eyes darted significantly to Will's.

"Let's start with when," Will suggested. "When, exactly, did all this happen?"

Lincoln nodded. He seemed to calm down. This time when he spoke, he spoke slowly and clearly.

"Four score and seven years ago," he intoned.

The Gettysburg Address. Lincoln was reciting the Gettysburg Address, the speech Abraham Lincoln delivered in the midst of America's bloody Civil War.

Lincoln grabbed Will's hand through the bars. He held it tightly.

"They want to assassinate me," he said. "But first they're assassinating my *character*." He leaned closer. "Don't believe a word you hear. I would never besmirch the office entrusted in me. Not the office of the presidency."

Will felt a wave of compassion flow through him. So

Lincoln believed he was *Abraham* Lincoln, the president who'd led the country in war, the president later killed by an assassin.

Lincoln was ill, that was clear. Mentally ill. He was not of sound mind, and he should be cared for somehow, watched over, as a parent would care for a sick child. But instead, he was living on the street. And now he'd been tossed into jail.

Will realized that there'd be no sense in sticking around, not at this point, no use trying to get any more information out of the man. He wished he could help Lincoln, but maybe the best help he could offer would be to get back to the office and make a few calls. He could find out the name of the lawyer assigned to Lincoln's case. He could call her up and make sure she knew to treat Lincoln with respect.

"I've led our nation to war," Lincoln said, shaking his head gravely. "A war that has rent one land in two. But I've had no choice in the matter, do you understand? No moral choice. No man should live enslaved."

"Of course not, Mr. President," said Will. He pressed Lincoln's hand. "History will absolve you."

"It's the elf!" Lincoln shouted, clasping Will's hand tighter. "He's the cause of all this misery!" He lowered his voice confidentially. "I captured him, you know," he whispered. "Yesterday. Beside the battlefield."

"You captured the elf?" asked Will.

"With my bare hands. But the devil is slippery. He escaped me. Though not before I snatched *this!*"

Lincoln ferreted something out of his pocket. The something was greenish. And brown. It was shaped like a cone, but it was soft and floppy.

"His hat!" crowed Lincoln. "Ha *ha!* I got the elf's hat! And what will he do without *that* in the winter months to come? Catch his death of a cold?"

Will stared. The hat was elf-sized. With camouflage colors. And a dirty little tassel at the tip. Exactly as Jack had described. . . .

"Could I see that?" he asked.

Lincoln handed it over.

"Mr. President," Will said respectfully, "do you mind if I hang on to this for a bit? I could use it, sir. You know, in my investigation."

"Of course," said Lincoln. "Intelligence. A president must always rely upon his intelligence. My agents are everywhere, stealthy as spies."

Will said good-bye, saluting Lincoln. He stuck the hat in his pocket and made his way back to Union Square. There, he found an empty bench and sat down. He took out the hat and looked at it.

The hat was tiny. No bigger than a doll's hat, really.

Of course, thought Will. That was it. The hat must be a doll's hat. Some kid probably dropped it outside the playground, and Lincoln must've picked it up.

But that didn't explain how Jack knew about it, did it?

Maybe Lincoln had been waving around the hat one day, and Jack had seen him. That was it. It was the only explanation that made any sense.

As Will looked out over the park, people were rushing past, people who might well pass that way every day. At one time or another, some of them had probably heard Lincoln shouting out about the elf, or even waving the hat. Though they wouldn't have paid him any attention.

But what difference was there really, Will wondered, between a homeless man ranting on about an elf, and a lot of so-called sane people throwing eggs at one another and going a little crazy in the park?

No wonder Jack wanted to believe in an elf. Who wouldn't want to believe in elves after all that had happened? Better to think that the trouble was caused by an elf than to think *people* could be so crazy.

Mimi was right, he thought. There's a part of us, some part in the heart of each one of us, that is not unlike a gnarled, spiteful little elf. What happened in the park the day before was proof enough of that.

Will stood up. Maybe he could write about that somehow, write about the events in the park and talk about why they'd happened. He could quote Jack—the child's perspective— and attribute the problems to the elf. "Nobody else could be so mean," Jack had said. "Nothing else can explain it."

Of course, nobody who read *The New York Times* would believe there actually *was* an elf. But it would move the reader, just as it had moved Will. It would get the reader thinking. And he could end the article with Jack's quote, the one about Gandhi.

"We could use the spirit of Gandhi here," the boy had said. "Now more than ever."

Will bounded down the stairs to the subway on his way back to *The Times.*

Later that day, unnoticed by the press, a fleet of trucks pulled into Union Square. The trucks were green, army green or nearly so, though on the side of each was stenciled a picture of a leaf, the logo of the Parks Department. A battalion of park workers piled out. The workers carried stacks of something, strange-looking cases molded of hard plastic, all black. Each of the cases had a hole at one end, a hole just big enough for a rat to squeeze through. And inside the hole, not visible to the eye or detectable in any way, was a dose of poison, rat poison. Rodenticide, as the Parks Department liked to call it.

"These babies oughta do the trick," one of the workers said, placing one of the cases under a tree. "Nice and dark, little holes . . . The rats'll go wild for this new design."

"Yeah," laughed another. "New and *improved.*"

The workers busied themselves distributing the traps. They set them all around the Square. At the edges of the lawn. In the bushes that bordered the playgrounds. And in the corners of the restaurant, now quiet. After that, they posted signs. CAUTION: RODENTICIDE! read the signs, warning people away.

The traps distributed, the signs posted, the workers returned to their trucks. They drove away.

A ghostly quiet settled over the Square.

16 A GRAVE MISTAKE

Early in the morning, just as the sun was waking to the day, Hiram woke up as well. He'd been holed up in the base of the flag-pole, asleep in his bed, and he'd been there for a while. Hiram wasn't sure how long he'd been holed up, but it might have been a couple of days. After the melee, he hadn't felt so well. He'd been feeling really achy and run-down. So he'd taken to his bed and stayed there.

Hiram remembered perfectly well the moment he'd first felt sick. It was the moment he'd shown himself to Jack. He'd felt a twinge in his stomach. And a wave of nausea. And though it's true that he had managed well enough to revel in the riot that followed, the real truth was, throughout the riot, he hadn't felt quite himself.

Now Hiram was worried. Worried that maybe something was wrong with him. Really wrong. Elves weren't supposed to show themselves to people, he knew that. The last time he'd been fool enough to let anyone see him, his father had cuffed him on the head, hard, knocking him clear across the room. And he'd yelled at him. Hiram could still hear his fa-ther's voice ringing in his ears.

"You brainless bonehead! What'sa matter with you? Are

you crazy or something? If you show yourself to a human, it'll make you sick! Or worse! All kindsa terrible things can happen. Any elf stupid enough to show himself is just asking for trouble. You gotta lie low, boy. You gotta keep out of the way of them people."

Over the years, Hiram never forgot what his father had told him. And he'd always done exactly as his father had advised. Of course, he'd let Lincoln see him, and more than once. But as anyone who spent any time in the park knew full well, Lincoln barely counted.

But maybe this Jack thing had been a mistake, a grave mistake.

Grave . . .

Hiram shuddered at the word.

What in the world had come over him? He knew he shouldn't have shown himself. And it wasn't just a quick glimpse he'd allowed. He'd let the boy stare straight at him for a full minute, maybe more. While he himself just stood there, grinning, as if the boy were no more than a tree stump. Or a toadstool.

Hiram grabbed the lost mitten that served as his pillow and clapped it over his head. Sleep . . . Sleep . . . If only he could sleep. . . .

Something jabbed him in the ribs. Something hard. And plastic.

A binky. A baby's binky. One from his collection, the binkies all littering the floor.

"One of these days, I gotta get this place cleaned up," he muttered.

"Hey," called a voice. "Anybody home?"

Whiskers twitched at the opening of Hiram's hole. It was Knut. He squeezed through the crack and shook out his fur.

"Whoa!" he said. "Did that crack get narrower, or did I gain a little weight here?" He smacked his lips, recalling the feast he'd had the night of the riot. All those fruits and vegetables rotting on the lawn!

"You know what I could really go for?" he mused. "Another hunk of that blueberry pie."

Hiram clutched his stomach. "Food?" he groaned. "Don't talk to me about food!"

"Why?" asked Knut. "What's the matter with you?"

"I ain't been feeling so good," Hiram told him.

Knut laid a paw on Hiram's forehead. It did feel a little warm.

"I should've figured something was up," said Knut. "I haven't seen you around since the big whoop-de-doo. I just figured you were staying home awhile, resting on your laurels."

"Naw," said Hiram. "I ain't got the strength to go out. I'm telling you. I been feeling lousy."

"There's something going around," said Knut. "A lot of the rats have been sick."

"They have?" asked Hiram.

"They say they feel all achy, real run-down."

Achy and run-down? Those were exactly Hiram's symptoms! Well, that was a relief. That must mean he had a bug, nothing more, that he hadn't done himself any real harm.

"Hey," said Knut, "I just realized. You've been holed up here, right? That means you haven't seen the park since the riot. Well, good news. It's going pretty much the way you predicted. There aren't a lot of people around. They're just starting to dribble back now."

"You don't say?" said Hiram. He roused himself and sat up in bed. He was beginning to feel better already.

"All that noise people made?" Knut laughed. "Looks like they scared themselves right off!"

Hiram wriggled into his shoes. Perhaps he should go outside, check things out. After all, he had a responsibility, didn't he? To himself. To the rats. To the welfare of the park as a whole.

"Come on," he said to Knut.

"Naw," said Knut. "Thanks anyway. I get sleepy this time of day, you know?"

Knut rested a paw on Hiram's bed. All those woolly hats and mittens, so soft and squishy—a ragbag of a bed! A rat could definitely get comfortable here.

"Hiram," Knut proposed. "I've got a favor to ask you."

"I don't do favors," snapped Hiram.

"Just a tiny one. Teensy tiny. I was thinking maybe I could hole up here awhile while you're out."

Hiram grunted.

"Does that mean yes?" Knut asked hopefully.

Hiram let out a breath, a long, slow breath. This was the trouble with having someone else hanging around. Exactly the trouble. Sooner or later, that someone always wanted something from you, always expected something.

"It means no way," snarled Hiram. "It means fat chance."

"Aw," Knut whined. He nosed the bed, the snug, comfy bed. "We're pals, remember? Not even a short while?"

The little rat stared at him with his beady little rat eyes.

"All right already," said Hiram. "A short while. But no longer."

Knut jumped onto the bed. "So what's your definition of 'a short while' exactly?"

"Let me put it this way. I better not find you here when I get back."

Hiram reached for his hat. If he was going out, he'd better get going. But the hat wasn't on the ledge where he usually kept it.

Oh. That's right, he'd forgotten. He didn't have his hat. Lincoln took it. He'd have to get it back.

Well, that shouldn't be too hard. Getting his hat back from Lincoln? Hiram chuckled.

That could even turn out to be fun. . . .

Outside, Hiram was pleased to see that the park looked much as Knut had described it. Not a lot of people. Mostly, Hiram noticed, it was just the regulars, and not even many of those. Hiram also noticed something else in the park. A bunch of plastic boxes set out in the grass. The boxes were black and had a hole at one end. They were tucked behind trees and into the corners of the fences. Probably, Hiram figured, they were someone's phony-baloney idea of an art exhibit. There was always some phony-baloney exhibit in the park. One year, someone had trucked in a bunch of statues of cows and set them around the grass. Cows! In New York City! Another year, somebody built a pyramid—twenty feet!—out of clay.

New Yorkers. *Ptooey!* Hiram spat. They were always looking to express themselves. He didn't give the boxes another thought.

Ah. But there was Celia. Hiram spotted her on a bench. She was sitting by herself, reading a newspaper. Hiram stole up behind her, climbed soundlessly up the splintery slats of the bench, and peered over her shoulder. The newspaper was folded open to an article by that reporter, that one who was always snooping around.

Celia was staring at the article. Suddenly, she broke down crying. She dropped her head into her hands and gave herself over completely to a surge of big, heaving sobs. Sobs that sounded as if a great well of sadness pooled up inside her was just now bursting free.

Hiram grinned. *Oh, yeah, baby!* There was nothing quite like the sight of a woman crying her eyes out to send a sweet tingle through an elf's chilly heart.

But suddenly, as quickly as Celia had broken into sobs, she stood up with great resolve. She wiped the tears from her cheeks, folded the newspaper, and strode over to Fare in the Square.

Fare in the Square was, of course, still closed. Shut down by edict of the mayor. But Mr. Porcini and Giovanni were there nonetheless, seated at a table, stubbornly reviewing a list of specials for the menu, as if the two were readying the place for business as usual.

Mr. Porcini flinched when he saw Celia.

That woman! That crazy woman! The one who'd thrown the pie at him! He threw up his hands to shield his face.

Celia raised her own hands high in the air. "Don't worry!" she called. "I'm unarmed!" And then, gruffly, awkwardly, she added, "I've come to apologize."

Apologize? Mr. Porcini wasn't sure he believed her. "You have?" he asked warily.

"I'm sorry," Celia told him. "I'm sorry I threw the broom at you."

"What about the pie?" he prompted.

"Of course," Celia hastened to add. "The pie, too. I'm sorry."

But Mr. Porcini was not about to let it go at that. Did this crazy lady think she could just stroll over and apologize, simple as that? Oh, no. As long as she'd come to beg his forgiveness, there were a few other questions he wanted answered.

"Why'd you do it?" he demanded. "Why'd you throw anything at me in the first place?"

Celia shrugged. "I don't know," she said. "What can I say? Something came over me. Something small. And mean." She thought of the article she'd read in the paper, the one Will had written, and her eyes welled again with tears. "I guess it's the elf inside me," she said, her voice going all quavery. "A mean-spirited little elf."

Giovanni let out a whoop. "Elf?" he cried. "You must be reading that article! It is just the same for me!"

Giovanni had only recently started reading *The New York*

Times. He still had to struggle to get through the articles, but he found it to be a very good exercise, one that helped his English—quite noticeably, he was sure. And that morning, when he'd come across Will's article, he'd found himself strangely moved.

"I am to be reading that article and reading it again," he said. He pounded his chest dramatically. "The elf? Inside here, he is. For what other cause are the peoples all running around fighting in our park?"

Despite Giovanni's patchy English, Celia knew what he meant. She knew exactly. He meant that he forgave her. Celia threw her arms around Giovanni and burst, again, into quick, hot tears.

"I'm sorry," she said. "I'm sorry," she repeated again and again.

With Celia dangling damply from his neck, Giovanni leaned over to Mr. Porcini and whispered something in his ear.

"What?" cried Mr. Porcini. "You've got to be kidding! Offer something like that? To her? Fat chance! The lady threw a *pie* at me!"

Giovanni whispered something again, and this time nudged his boss. Mr. Porcini let out a long sigh. In his heart he knew Giovanni was right.

"Oh," he grumbled. "All right. Celia," he started. "That is your name, isn't it?"

Celia nodded, sniffing back tears.

"Here we are, neighbors in the park," said Mr. Porcini,

"and it's a shame that we've never officially met before. We certainly appreciate all the work you do. I mean, what *do* you do here? Keep up the park? Keep it clean?"

Celia narrowed her eyes.

"What I mean to say," Mr. Porcini stumbled on, "is how'd you like to come to lunch sometime? At Fare in the Square? As my guest?"

Celia glanced around the restaurant, which was closed. Clearly. Was Mr. Porcini making a bad joke?

"Obviously," Mr. Porcini hastened to add, "we're shut down right now. So I can't give you a firm date on the invitation. But we're bound to reopen, and when we do, it'll be a very happy occasion. I hope I can count on you to join us for the celebration."

Lunch? At Fare in the Square? As the guest of Mr. Porcini? This is what Celia had imagined so many times— though always with a twinge, the stubborn feeling that the thing she wished for would never come true.

"I'd love to," Celia said.

Mr. Porcini looked down at the table and doodled on the list with his pen. "I'm only sorry I never asked you before," he admitted.

Giovanni wiped a tear from his own eye.

"This is too sadness," he said. He pounded on his chest again. "The elf? The elf, he cause too much pains."

Just then, Giovanni looked up. He'd noticed a sound. The sound of children arriving at the playground next door. One voice, a familiar voice, sounded above all the others.

Giovanni leaped from the table, where Mr. Porcini was now reading Celia the list of specials they'd planned.

"I must to go!" Giovanni announced abruptly.

And with no more fare-thee-well than that, he ran across the street to the deli.

Inside the deli, Giovanni peered into the pastry case, his face eager and expectant. Displayed inside the case among all the cakes and crullers, the brownies and buns, were some cookies. Giovanni's eye strayed to one in particular, a very large one. It was shaped like an animal.

A puppy! A frisky little pup! *Perfetto!* The cookie was thickly smeared with chocolate icing, with a pearly dollop of vanilla for an eye.

"One puppy, please," Giovanni said, pointing to the cookie.

Flawless. Giovanni beamed. His English was flawless. . . .

The clerk behind the counter wrapped the cookie in a bag. Giovanni raced back to the park, to the playground, where he stood a moment inside the gate, watching.

Christopher was running from one end of the playground to the other and then back again. He was running so fast, it looked almost as if a dam had burst inside him, a dam that had held back all the energy the poor boy had had to keep in check all those days he'd been kept away.

Giovanni stepped in front of him.

"Hey!" Christopher protested.

Giovanni handed him the bag.

"I'm sorry I yell at you," he apologized. "I'm sorry I say mean things, that I boot out you from restaurant."

Christopher tore open the bag and pulled out the cookie. "Wow!" he said. "Is this for me?"

Giovanni nodded.

And then Christopher did an unusual thing—unusual, that is, for a child who's been handed a cookie. He broke it in half and handed part to Giovanni.

Now, it's possible that Christopher did this because he was a twin. Twins are often called upon to share. Many's the time Christopher had watched Hyacinth break a sweet in two and divvy up the pieces, half to himself and half to his sister. Still, it was a generous gesture for Christopher to make. Though it must be admitted that he did examine both pieces before he handed one to Giovanni. The head half or the tail half?

He handed over the tail.

Which was as close to an apology as he might be expected to make.

Giovanni grinned. "Thank yee, *pahdner,*" he drawled, a little something he'd heard in a movie once. An American movie. Cowboy. He bit off a chunk of the puppy's tail. "Yee-haw!" he cried.

And then, as if he were goading a pony, Giovanni gave a slap to his rear. *Giddyup!* He galloped off toward the monkey bars, where he jumped up, grabbed hold of a rung, and swung there by an arm.

Will laughed when he saw Giovanni swinging from the monkey bars. For Will had come back to the park that day, too. And he'd peeked into the playground when he'd heard the clutch of children there, shouting and laughing. Truth be told, Will was feeling pretty frisky himself that morning. He had just mailed off an envelope to Mimi and Jack, and in the envelope he'd stuck a check for a hundred dollars to cover the fine he'd brought upon them. He'd also enclosed a letter he'd written, apologizing for his behavior. Which made him feel lighter than air.

Will waved to Giovanni. Giovanni waved back.

Hiram, watching the scene, the whole, happy scene, was irritated no end.

"Happy, *schmappy!*" he muttered.

Oh, it had been a bad morning for Hiram. He'd come outside with high hopes, imagining the best, by which he meant the worst. After what Knut had told him (just *wait'll* he got a hold of that Knut!), he had hoped to see the park in a shambles, the people bitter and defeated. Instead, he had to watch a lot of goodwill circulating, a lot of people smiling, wasn't that sweet?, a lot of people making their little apologies.

"Sorry?" he muttered. "I'll show you sorry. This park is in one sorry state!"

Swiftly and soundlessly, Hiram stole into the sandbox and kicked up a cloud of sand. As people shielded their eyes against the grit, he grabbed a pile of toys, snatching a red plastic shovel from a little girl's fist, and dropped the lot in front of Christie, who sat splay-legged and surprised as the sand settled around her.

Christie picked up the shovel. The other girl sent up a wail. Ginger glanced over and saw her daughter presiding over the pile.

"What a *good* little girl you are," she said, puffing with pride. "Now you have *all* the toys!"

Hiram grinned. Oh, yeah! He could always count on Ginger.

Though the other mother quickly retrieved the shovel and handed it back—"There you go"—comforting the girl who was crying, and drying her tears.

Hiram had seen enough. He had work to do. Important work. He had to get his hat back from Lincoln. He might as well get cracking at that now.

Hiram didn't have to look far to find Lincoln. Lincoln, returned that morning from jail, had posted himself in his usual spot. But as Hiram approached, he saw someone else there, someone talking to Lincoln. Hiram moved closer to investigate.

That reporter! Why, that big buttinsky! What'd he think, he owned the park? Always poking his nose here, there, poking his big, fat nose everywhere it didn't belong. Him and his articles, his snoopy, meddling articles, those articles that got everybody all misty-eyed, all gooey-hearted. Articles that sabotaged every one of Hiram's well-laid plans.

Hiram crept closer, scouting out a place to hide. He spied one of those boxes—all black, of course, arty-farty if ever he saw it—that were scattered all around the park, and he slipped behind it. From there he could see Will and what he was up to. Will was digging into his pocket. He pulled out something. Hiram squinted. What was it?

Great galloping rat attack! It was his cap! How in the world had that reporter gotten his cap?

145

Why, that no-good Lincoln! He must've handed over the cap easy as you please! What a blabbermouth! By now, he'd probably told the reporter all about him. Not that Lincoln hadn't been shouting the news to everybody and his uncle for some time now. But this time, he'd handed over evidence, to boot. Which meant that somebody might actually *believe* him.

Oh, this was dandy! Now that that pesky reporter knew about him, he'd probably start looking for Hiram, trying to track him down. Hiram would have to lie low, even lower than usual.

Will tucked the hat back in his pocket and started to walk away. Uh-oh! He was heading straight toward Hiram. Hiram ducked into the hole at one end of the black box. Inside, it was dark, as dark as the wrong end of a sinkhole. But as his eyes adjusted, Hiram saw something, a little pan of something, something that looked like pellets, maybe they were pellets of food. He sniffed them.

And then his heart sank.

Rat poison! The black boxes were full of rat poison!

"A lot of the rats have been feeling sick," Knut had told him. *"They say they feel all achy, real run-down."*

Hiram wriggled out of the box and peered up. There, posted on the fence above him, he saw a sign that broadcast the news.

CAUTION: RODENTICIDE!

Of course! Why hadn't he seen it before? What had he been thinking? Hiram sprinted back toward the flagpole, his stunted little legs flashing in the sun.

"Knut!" he cried. "The black boxes! They're poison!"

He squeezed into his hole and clicked on the flashlight. He tore off the covers of his bed, looking frantically around.

But the hole was empty.

Knut had already gone.

17 A CONTAGION OF KINDNESS

Will stood outside the door, staring at the buzzer. CRAIN, it read. This was the place, all right. When Will pressed the buzzer, Mimi swung open the door.

"Hi," she said brightly. And then, calling toward the back of the apartment, "Jack! Will's here!"

Mimi invited Will in. "Jack was thrilled when you quoted him in your article," she told him. "It really meant a lot to him."

Will glanced around. The apartment was cozy. Well, cozy was one word for it. Cramped was another. And cluttered. Definitely cluttered. Will was standing in the kitchen, which was really just a stove and a sink and a refrigerator against one wall. The table across from it, an old, knotty pine, was piled high with newspapers and mail. Will was glad to notice, on top of the pile, the envelope he'd sent them.

"Excuse the mess," Mimi said apologetically. "If I had anywhere else to put all this stuff, believe me, I would." She noticed Will's eye on the envelope. "Thanks a lot for your note, by the way," she added. "And the money, of course. It was really thoughtful of you to send it."

The cat crawled out from under the couch and nuzzled his head against Will's ankles.

Jack came bounding into the room.

"So what exactly are you two doing today?" Mimi asked.

"Skateboarding, Mom," said Jack. He grinned mischievously. "Among other things."

"We'll be looking for the elf," Will explained. He winked at Mimi as he said this, though he was careful not to let Jack see.

"The elf, huh?" said Mimi.

"And speaking of the elf . . . ," he said.

He pulled the elf's hat out of his pocket.

"Wow!" cried Jack. "That's it! The elf's hat! How did you get it?"

"The elf's hat?" Mimi repeated. She was frowning, a look of concern clouding her face.

"Lincoln gave it to me," said Will. "He told me he grabbed it off the elf when the two of them got into a tussle." Will looked again significantly at Mimi. "It looks like a doll's hat, though, doesn't it? I mean, anyone who's not in the know would *assume* that's what it was. I know I would. But apparently it belongs to the elf."

Mimi glanced at Jack.

"Jack," she said, "you're not going skateboarding without your helmet."

"Oops."

As Jack ran back to his room to fetch his helmet, Mimi leaned toward Will and lowered her voice. "I have to say, it's been worrying me that Jack thinks he saw an elf."

"Aw," said Will, "I wouldn't worry about it."

"But don't you think he's a little old for that kind of thing?"

"Nah. It's refreshing, really. A kid who wants to go hunting for elves in the park rather than sit hunched over a video game?"

"I guess so," said Mimi. "But whenever he talks about the elf, I don't know quite what to say."

"Look," Will assured her. "It's a kid's job to believe in elves, and it's a mom's job to worry. Sounds to me like you're both right on track."

Jack ran back into the room, fastening his helmet. Will handed him the hat.

"Here," he said. "Why don't you be the keeper of the cap?"

"Really?"

"Sure. Put it in your backpack. That'd be the best place for it. That way, we'll have it with us if we come across the elf."

"When," Jack corrected him. "Not if."

Will and Jack had planned their trip to the park that day as a special holiday outing. Because that day was Labor Day, the last day of summer. Traditionally, on Labor Day weekend New Yorkers flee the city. They travel to the beach, or to the country, for one last fling with freedom before September officially gets under way. But the people who do stay in town flock to the parks. And Union Square was no exception. By now, people had begun filtering back, lots of people, more than just the regulars. For people in New York City cannot stay away from their parks for very long.

"Look," said Will, pointing to a bare, torn-up patch of ground. It was the spot where the statue of Gandhi usually stood. Now a bulldozer was parked there. The bulldozer was idle in observance of the holiday, but displayed on the front of it, hung on the hood, was a lei of fresh, fragrant flowers.

"Gandhi may be gone," Will observed, "but his friends are still around."

Jack skated ahead, stopping near a tree.

"This is where I saw the elf," he called back.

He dropped to his knees to examine the ground. He found a couple of sticks. And some rocks. And a nasty old gum wrapper, that was all. He'd been hoping for footprints. Elf footprints. Wait a minute. Those were some prints there in the dirt, weren't they?

"What do you think?" he asked Will.

"Squirrel tracks," declared Will. "Or pigeon. Unless this elf has a mighty strange foot."

The two continued to search the park. They searched behind the benches and by the low stone curbs that bordered the walkways. Jack was hoping the elf had lost something, an item of clothing, perhaps, one he might have abandoned somehow. Carelessly. A shoe with turned-up toes, for instance. Or a lone camouflage sock to pair with the cap. But that day, they found nothing of the sort. Just some acorns and bottle caps and lots of scraps of garbage. Nothing to indicate that an elf had ever been there at all.

"Hey, Jack," beckoned Will. "Look at this."

A woman on a bench was eating a bagel. She'd torn it in half, and as they watched, offered a portion to the gentleman sitting next to her. That gentleman tore off a piece of his share and shared it with the pigeons who pecked hungrily nearby.

Jack screwed up his face. "What is it?" he asked. "Some kind of evidence?"

"The opposite, I'd say," said Will. "I mean, in a way of thinking. It's people being nice to each other."

"Oh," Jack said, disappointed.

"Hey!" Will exclaimed. "Will you look at that! People are actually smiling at each other!"

"Where?" said Jack.

"There. And there, too. Everywhere, actually."

It was true. All through the park, strangers were smiling—even waving!—as they passed one another on the walkways. Adults were smiling at children. People without dogs were smiling at those with. Small expressions of kindness and friendliness seemed to be cropping up all over. Like buds poking their heads up through a newly sun-warmed soil.

Jack frowned. He got out his notebook. He wrote down the places in the Square he'd searched so far. Tree beds. Check. Benches. Check. Curbsides. Check. Where should he look next?

Will turned to Jack. "It's remarkable, isn't it?" he said. "The change in people lately?"

"I guess so," Jack said sullenly.

Will studied him carefully. "What's the matter?" he asked. "You disappointed?"

Jack nodded.

"That we haven't found any clues about the elf?"

"Yeah," Jack admitted. "I mean, I was hoping for a sock or something. I was sure I'd find *footprints.*" Jack sighed. He didn't want to say the next part, but he was thinking that Will might be right. That with everyone in the park walking around all smiles and acting so nice to each other, the elf seemed far away indeed.

"Don't worry," Will consoled him. "We'll find the elf. Remember, we just started looking. We can't expect to find anybody as wily as he is our first time out."

A dog pulled at his leash and licked the face of a little girl sitting in a stroller. She giggled.

"Looks like happiness is contagious," said Will.

He took a seat on one of the benches that lined the walkway. Jack stowed his board and sat beside him.

"Just the same as meanness," Jack observed.

"Speaking of which," said Will. He was grinning. "I've got something for you."

"You do?" Jack asked. "What is it?"

Will handed Jack a small package. "Guess you'll have to open it up and see," he said.

Jack tore open the paper.

"Wow!" he crowed. "An Avenger's Revenge cartridge!"

"I figured I owed it to you," said Will. "After all, I blew your chances for ever having another lemonade stand. At least in Union Square."

Jack smiled hesitantly at Will, at a loss, suddenly, for anything to say.

It was right at this moment that Hiram came upon them.

Hiram was in the park searching for Knut. A terrible question gnawed at him. Why had he turned away his friend?

Friend? he asked himself. Is that what Knut was?

Why didn't I let him stay? he wondered. Why couldn't I do him that favor?

Not being able to find Knut had put Hiram in a foul temper. And so when he came upon Will and Jack, when he saw that Will had given Jack a present and that Jack had gone all hungry-eyed in response, his expression twisted. Twisted up like an old rag wrung dry.

"Well, isn't that just sweet?" he scoffed.

Jack was smiling shyly at Will. Will broke the silence.

"So," he said. "Shouldn't you and I be off again? To look for that elf?"

Look for that elf?

A shower of crumbs fell on Will. He looked around. Where had they come from? There was no one else around.

"No one but *that elf,*" Hiram muttered to himself. "And fat chance you're gonna find me."

He slipped back into the cover of the brush. He still had to try to find Knut.

Ahead in the dirt, Hiram spied something. A rat, it looked like. The rat was just lying there, quiet, still, as if he had fallen into a lazy-day snooze. Was it Knut? Hiram hurried to see. It wasn't likely to be Knut, he told himself. Not out in the daytime. That wouldn't be like Knut at all.

Hiram turned the rat over and peered at its face. Just as he'd predicted. It wasn't Knut. Which was lucky, very lucky.

Because the rat that Hiram came upon was stiff. And stone-cold.

Dead.

Hiram shuddered.

The first rat that he'd come upon who'd died from the powerful new poison.

18 THE RATS' LAST RALLY

By nightfall, more rats had died. Their carcasses lay strewn lifelessly all about the lawn in Union Square, like so many bodies scattered on a battlefield. Hiram rushed from one to the next, checking each body. Was it Knut? Not this one. Nor the next. Hiram could only think that Knut must've crawled off somewhere, crawled off into some hole to die.

Hiram was angry. He gave himself a thorough tongue-lashing. He called himself a moron, a dunce, whatsamatter with you, you blockhead? Why hadn't he been able to find and warn his only friend?

As night fell, there were few left to witness what would happen. Only Hiram and some rats. And the moon, of course, hanging high above the scene, casting its eerie glow.

The rats who were left milled about on the lawn among the bodies of their fellows. This was the lawn, they recalled, where they'd gathered before, on a happier night, a more hopeful night, the night Hiram had stood before them and addressed them, the night he had led them out as one.

Hiram . . .

The elf's name clanged loudly in their ears.

Now the rats gathered in an anxious knot. They had yet to come up with a plan.

"What can we do?" asked one, voicing the concern of them all.

The old rat, the scrawny one with sparse whiskers and patchy fur, emerged from the jumble and spoke loudly.

"We have to leave the park," he said.

"No!" cried another. "The park is our home!"

"*Was* our home," said the old rat. "We can't stay here. Not with the Black Death plaguing us. By now all of you know not to venture into those cases, but what about your children?"

Those rats who had children with them shepherded them closer. So the young ones wouldn't wander off, wouldn't be tempted by the pretty poison.

"Those black cases," the old rat continued, "contain the deadliest poison to be used against us yet, a poison that delivers a slow death, but a certain one, a death that is prolonged and gruesome."

The crowd kept their eyes trained on the rat who spoke, none of them wanting to look at the lawn around them, a lawn littered with the bodies of their fellows.

"But where?" asked one. "Where will we go?"

"There are places," said the old rat. "Places near here where we can try to find food, hope for some shelter."

He paused.

"But we must spread out," he said. "Split up."

A murmur spread through the crowd. Split up? This was something they hadn't considered. Did he really expect them to leave not only their homes, but their families, their friends, their neighbors? These rats had grown up together, been children together, borne children of their own.

They'd nursed their sick together . . .

Sick who were now dead.

"But wouldn't it be better to go as a group?" asked one. "We'd have strength in numbers."

The old rat shook his head. "Where could we go that would be big enough for all of us? There's no place near here that's as spacious as the Square. But we'll survive," he said.

The others did not look certain.

"We will," he assured them. "We're resourceful. We're rats."

The rats clustered together in one disheartened mass. And then, as one, they began to make their way out of the park. Once they had left the park, they would split up. They would have to. But for now they walked together. One last time.

It was then that they stumbled upon Hiram.

Hiram was bent over the body of a rat in the lawn, a rat not Knut. But where was Knut? Hiram wondered. Why couldn't he find him? Something choked his throat, something sharp and hard. Something that wouldn't dissolve, wouldn't break up.

Something with no way to escape.

"So there you are."

Hiram looked up. The old rat who'd addressed him stood next to him, staring at him. Around him were more rats. A small crowd.

Hiram stood up and returned their stares. Defiantly.

"You seen Knut?" he asked.

"If he's not with us?" said the old rat. He nodded at the bodies on the lawn.

The rest was left unspoken.

"You led us astray," said the old rat.

Hiram sneered. "Ha! I ain't led you nowhere you weren't itching to go yourselves."

"You promised us the world," said the old rat. "You promised us the *park*."

"So take it," said Hiram, gesturing grandly. "You see anybody here stopping you?"

"The park isn't safe for us any longer," said the old rat. "You know that. The people didn't flee as you said they would. They didn't leave the park to us. They left us another surprise."

"Oh, no," protested Hiram. "You ain't pinning that on me. I ain't the one laid the traps."

"Look at the lawn," said the old rat. "Look at the bodies here. This is what you delivered to us. Death."

The old rat took a step closer. The other rats surrounded Hiram, closing in. They squeaked, a high, keening squeak.

Hiram broke through the ranks and waggled his fingers in his ears. "Come and get me," he taunted. He gave the old rat a quick slap on his rump. "Tag! You're it!"

Hiram took off, sprinting across the grass. The rats chased after him.

They chased him across the lawn. And through the links of the fence.

They chased him past the shrubbery.

And down the steps of the Square.

Then into the street, to the middle of the—

Screech!

A lone taxi trolling the avenue for late-night fares skid-
ded to a stop.

The rats ran on, scattering.

Away from the park.

Up onto the sidewalks.

A score of shifting shadows.

Day broke. The moon went to bed, taking with it its secrets,
the secret of the rats and their last rally, of all it had wit-
nessed during the night. The sun woke up brash and brassy,
determined to shed a stronger light. And to illuminate what
needed to be done.

By 6:00 A.M., Celia's staff arrived for work. That morning,
there was no dog poop for them to clean up; there hadn't
been for a while now. But the workers faced a grizzlier task.
They had to dispose of the bodies. All those stiff, fright-faced
rats.

The workers put on gloves. They handed out shovels and
large plastic garbage bags, the tough, heavy-duty kind. They
spread out throughout the Square, scooping up the bodies of
the dead and dropping them unceremoniously into their
bags.

Cleaning up the carcasses. Carcasses of dead rats.

As if the bodies were little more than a nuisance.

Nothing more than leaves fallen off the trees in autumn.

19 THE WINDS OF CHANGE

Fall tinged the air. The breeze had a bit of a bite to it. In New York City this often happens after Labor Day. The weather changes, taking a turn toward the cool. As if whoever's up there regulating the weather has turned the page of a calendar, has noticed that it's soon to be fall, and has decided to provide a hint of the new season. A promise of the weather to come.

September. The month had arrived. The month Hiram had said would mark the downfall of the park, the one by which he'd predicted that all would've changed for the worse.

And things in the park had changed, all right. Though not in Hiram's favor. This crisp September morning, construction vehicles crowded the park, the renovation proceeding merrily. The restaurant, temporarily closed, had now been slated to reopen. The reopening was scheduled for that day, in fact, for one last hurrah before it shuttered back down for the fall.

Celia had been invited to the celebratory lunch. As had Parks Commissioner Greene—who had at last okayed the renewal of the restaurant's lease.

And so it was that Mr. Porcini and Giovanni were now scurrying about, making preparations. The two were headed to the Greenmarket to shop for produce. For the Greenmarket had also been cleared to reopen that day. A turn of events that everyone in the park had been very pleased to hear.

Changes. So many changes. The winds of change were nipping the air.

That morning, Jack and Mimi, too, passed through Union Square. They were hurrying toward the subway, where once again (after a more eventful summer than either one of them would have ever expected) they were headed to work and to school.

The first day of school this time, not the last.

"Hey, buddy!" called a voice. They stopped. It was Will. He clapped Jack on his backpack. "So you're off to school again, are you?"

"Yup," said Jack. And then, voicing the concern that had been worrying him, "Which means I'm not going to have as much time to spend looking for . . ." He glanced around. "You know, the elf."

"Oh, don't worry about him," Will assured him. "I'm on the case." He aimed a discreet wink at Mimi. "That elf can hide, but he won't escape. I'll smoke him out. I'm a reporter, don't forget. An investigative reporter."

A cloud of dust blew up in Will's face, setting him blinking. A cloud of dust kicked up by someone unseen, someone nearby, someone crouched under the slats of a park bench.

Hiram.

Who had returned to the park. Unharmed by the rats.

Or by the deadly tread of a taxi's tires.

Hiram sneered.

Smoke me out, eh? he thought. So what's this guy want to do now? Write another article about me? Every Tom, Dick, and Harry'll flock to Union Square to go elf hunting, thinking it's the latest sport. Or maybe he thinks he's gonna catch me himself, hold me high for everybody to see, like some kinda trophy.

Well, think again, newsboy.

It was at this point that Hiram found himself thinking along new lines altogether.

That fool can look for me all he wants. He can scour every inch of the park. But he ain't gonna find me, is he?

Not if I ain't here. . . .

This last thought surprised Hiram, who had not known he'd been about to make such a big decision. Leave the park, the park that had long been his home? Sure. Why not? He'd go someplace else. Who needed Union Square, anyway? It hadn't exactly turned into the place of his dreams.

A few feet away, Jack fidgeted. His mom had taken a tissue to Will's eyes, helping him wipe out the dust. *Sheesh!* Could his mom be any more embarrassing? And now she'd started talking to him. Oh, great. Once she got talking, there was no stopping her. Why was Will even bothering to listen? Will was *his* friend, not hers.

"Come on, Mom," Jack said impatiently. He tugged at her sleeve. "We'll be late."

As Mimi talked on, Jack dropped to a bench to sit down. He unzipped his backpack. Where was that granola bar he'd packed as a snack? This looked like as good a time as any to eat it. . . .

"Jack!" cried Mimi. She'd noticed, suddenly, that her son was sitting down. "What are you doing? Get up. We've got to catch the subway. We'll be late."

"What do you think I've been *telling* you?"

At that time of morning the subway station was crowded. Mimi and Jack pushed through the people and onto the platform.

"Mom," said Jack, peering down at the tracks. "Look. A rat."

Mimi shuddered and pulled Jack back, away from the edge of the platform.

"Hiram!" cried a voice, a voice they did not hear.

Hiram jumped onto the platform and threaded his way through the forest of legs planted there. He neared the edge and peered over. Who was calling him?

"Over here!" cried the voice.

Could it be? It was Knut! He was alive! And in the subway! Down on the tracks!

"Knut!" cried Hiram, his eyes misting. "I thought you were—"

"Yeah, yeah, I know. But I got myself some street smarts hanging out with you, didn't I? That poison trick? Fat chance I was gonna fall for that. Hey," said Knut, noticing. "You got your hat back. Where'd you find it?"

Hiram nodded across the platform toward Jack. "Somebody's backpack," he said. "I hitched a ride."

"So what are you doing down here?" asked Knut.

"Flying the coop, what else? Saving my skin."

"Well, come on down. You can bunk with me. You'll like it here. Plenty of noise and confusion."

"Nah. I gotta hop the next train outta here. I'm gonna go as far as it'll take me."

"No. Don't tell me. You're leaving Union Square?"

Hiram nodded.

"Well, isn't that a kicker. Where are you going?"

"Listen," said Hiram. "Knut—"

He wanted to tell Knut something, something he had been thinking.

"Yeah?"

"I just want to tell you—"

But the words stuck in his throat, hard to say.

"So spit it out already."

"I just wanted to say . . ." Hiram swallowed. Hard. "I just wanted to tell you to lie low. That's it. And stay outta the way of them people, you know what I'm saying? Or all kindsa terrible things can happen."

Knut nodded solemnly. "Tell me about it," he said.

A rumbling sound shook the platform. Muffled at first, then louder. A train was careering toward the station. Knut scuttled under a rail, taking cover against the sharp, glinting wheels.

"See you, Hiram!" he called back. "So long! And good luck!"

The train pulled in. The doors opened. People jammed in, pushing and shoving. Jack crammed into the car and shouldered up to a pole. A voice came over the intercom, garbled and crackly, the announcement barely audible.

"Ladies and gentlemen, this train is going to *Khmzhsvnn*. The next station will be *Xmzhvkrsk*. All *hgfwsxz* wishing to go to *Qxvmnpz* should *fqmtrwk* at *khgftpb*."

The people in the car turned to each other anxiously. "What did he say?" they asked. "Are we skipping the next stop? Is this train going express?"

Jack reached into his backpack. The ride would take a while. Maybe this would be a good time to get out that granola bar.

Hmm. That was funny. The wrapper was open. And it looked as if someone had already eaten some. He didn't remember eating any of it back in the park. . . .

Jack took a bite.

The train rumbled out of the station, picking up speed.

It screeched through the tunnel.

And into September.

Leaving Union Square and all the strange things that had happened there that summer far, far behind.